# KEANE

## The Mavericks, Book 09

# Dale Mayer

KEANE: THE MAVERICKS, BOOK 9
Beverly Dale Mayer
Valley Publishing Ltd.



ISBN-13: 978-1-773362-97-7
Print Edition

# About This Book

What happens when the very men—trained to make the hard decisions—come up against the rules and regulations that hold them back from doing what needs to be done? They either stay and work within the constraints given to them or they walk away. Only now, for a select few, they have another option:

The Mavericks. A covert black ops team that steps up and break all the rules … but gets the job done.

Welcome to a new military romance series by *USA Today* best-selling author Dale Mayer. A series where you meet new friends and just might get to meet old ones too in this raw and compelling look at the men who keep us safe every day from the darkness where they operate—and live—in the shadows … until someone special helps them step into the light.

**Heading out on a last-ditch rescue mission to Puget Sound one day after two women go overboard in a sailing accident isn't exactly what he'd expected …**

But Keane is nothing if not adaptable. He can only hope the two women are alive and doing everything they can to stay that way. Hearing from the local coast guard that more may be involved than just a rescue mission, he and his partner load up and head out to search the waters around the smaller islands off the coast. They have the GPS of the missing women's last-known location, but storms could have sent them anywhere …

Lost, alone—except for her best friend, who's unconscious with a head wound—Sandrine wakes up in a small shelter to find they are locked in. When the door is finally opened, an armed stranger dressed in fatigues dumps a small amount of food and says they are on their own.

Finding the women was one thing, keeping them safe something else again. More is going on in this small island that any of them were expecting … or had planned for …

**Sign up to be notified of all Dale's releases here!**

https://geni.us/DaleNews

## Books in This Series

Kerrick, Book 1

Griffin, Book 2

Jax, Book 3

Beau, Book 4

Asher, Book 5

Ryker, Book 6

Miles, Book 7

Nico, Book 8

Keane, Book 9

Lennox, Book 10

Gavin, Book 11

Shane, Book 12

Diesel, Book 13

Jerricho, Book 14

Killian, Book 15

Hatch, Book 16

Corbin, Book 17

Aiden, Book 18

Boxed Sets and Bundles

https://geni.us/Bundlepage

# CHAPTER 1

A WEEK LATER, Keane Lytton walked down Fisherman's Wharf in Seattle. The place was jam-packed with people, and he wondered what the hell he was doing here. Surely there was a better place for a meeting. Of course, if you want to get lost in a crowd, this was the place to be. It was overcast with a threat of rain. Still, he couldn't, for the life of him, imagine why he was here. But somebody with greater wisdom had decided this, and so a meetup was needed. He walked down the pier where he was expected, and, as he found the spot, he sat and turned his back on the crowd behind him.

Charlotte and Nico had holed up in Charlotte's house for the last few days, and Keane had been more than happy to take a break. He was eager to join the Mavericks with his own mission to head up and had listened to stories about many other ops from the others who had gone before him. He was okay with that. He was just waiting for it to happen.

When a hand landed on his shoulder, he turned in surprise and looked up to see Lennox staring at him. Keane's eyebrows shot up. "Man, am I glad to see you."

"Good," Lennox said. "Are you willing to work with me too?" He held up an envelope. "We've got orders."

Keane and Lennox sat on the side of the wharf, while the noise of the crowd around them completely faded away.

Keane said, "I was given very little information on it."

"That's because very little is to be had," Lennox admitted. "I've never been on a mission with less information."

"So, what do we know?"

"A group of people went out for a day of sailing. Two of them were washed overboard."

"And the coast guard didn't find them?" Keane asked, staring at Lennox in surprise. "Not terribly unusual, I suppose, given the size of the search area."

Lennox replied, "The coast guard and private yachts haven't seen any sign of them."

"The currents, depending on where they were at the time, could have taken the bodies to any number of places."

"Well, they went missing in Puget Sound," Lennox said.

"Seriously? Puget Sound is interconnected to multiple waterways and basins, not to mention the Pacific Ocean. The currents can change and can run really deep," Keane said. "A search like that involves any number of issues. They may never be found."

"Exactly," Lennox said. "In this case a special request has been made for us to look for them."

Keane gazed at the long lampposts that dotted the pier. "Are you serious?"

Lennox gave him half a grin. "Never more so."

"What? We're in the business of looking for bodies now?" he asked incredulously. "I was expecting to go up against a serial killer or work in the midst of a civil war in a dictator-ruled country or God-only-knows-what, but you're saying my mission is to look for two bodies?" Turning, Keane stared at the water. "Not only that, it's almost impossible to succeed at a job like this."

"Only a couple reasons explain why we're doing this,"

Lennox said, lowering his voice.

"Of course," Keane said. "It's got to be the daughter or niece or nephew to somebody pretty high up the line."

"An admiral," Lennox said. "His daughter and her friend."

"Has he been looking personally?"

"No. He's out on the Baltic Sea, but he's been calling in every favor he could."

"And so a special black-ops mission team of two is to go out into Puget Sound, and possibly beyond into the Pacific Ocean, and look for them?"

"Yes," Lennox replied.

Just then Keane's phone buzzed in his pocket, and he pulled it out to see Nico was calling. Keane lifted the phone to his ear. "Hope you have a better explanation as to why I'm supposed to look for two bodies," Keane snapped.

"So Lennox already told you about the admiral's daughter?"

"Absolutely, but what does this have to do with us? What's wrong with search and rescue, the coast guard or a private recovery company?"

"Because," he said, "they went missing from the same area where two other people went missing just one week ago. Both pairs somewhere in the same area. Plus, we received a distress call from one of those first two who went missing, saying they'd been captured."

# CHAPTER 2

KEANE SLOWLY STRAIGHTENED. "Captured?"

"Yes," Nico said briskly. "Bodies showed up a few days later, both shot. So we don't know exactly what the hell we've got going on here."

"What islands are around their last-known locations? How about any permanent houseboats? Hell, what about speedboats passing through here? Just what the hell is going on?"

"We don't know," Nico said. "But once the admiral heard about his daughter, he asked for a team to be brought in."

"Of course he did," Keane said, staring at the water in front of them. "Puget Sound is full of islands. Most of them uninhabited. About 99 percent I would say," he said.

"That we know of," Nico corrected. "The fact of the matter is, we have narrowed it down to the closest four islands, where we know these latest two women were washed off the boat."

"Washed off in a storm or helped off?" Keane asked.

"Well, that's one of the questions. Two men were on the boat with them—they both survived," he said. They're not saying much though. Only that a really bad storm came, and the women were washed overboard."

"Life jackets?"

"Yes."

"And how long ago?"

"Yesterday morning."

"Well, if they're still in the water, they're dead," Keane snapped. "Hypothermia would have set in very quickly, and it doesn't matter what kind of life jacket they've got on. It won't keep them afloat for all that long, particularly if they're dead."

"We all know that, including the admiral. Especially the admiral. But, if the slightest chance remains that his daughter is alive out there, he wants to exhaust every avenue. The fact that we had a distress call after the prior incident, saying that first couple were captured, expands the potential scenarios."

"And makes no sense at all. It's not like we have pirates here," Keane said, interested in spite of himself. "I guess I could do a whole lot worse than spending a few days on a boat looking for someone."

"Less on a boat, more on the islands," Nico said. "Another thing I can tell you is that some research is going on in that area."

"What kind of research?" Keane asked, looking at Lennox, who was listening in on the call.

"Top secret," Nico replied.

"So, a top secret installation is on one of these freaking islands, near where two people disappeared a week ago and two more disappeared yesterday morning. Those most recent two are probably in the ocean, but, because of this installation and because of the distress call, you're afraid it may be something far more sinister."

"Exactly," Nico said. I can't give you too many details because we just don't have them. Apparently this research center involves a couple other countries, as well."

"Don't tell me—Russia, China, or both?"

"No, not necessarily. It's somehow in conjunction with Japan."

"Well, we are allies."

"They're not saying that the installation itself is in the wrong hands or that it's operating illegally," Nico continued. "Or that it even has anything to do with these missing people," he said. "The other thing is that this installation isn't manned all the time. It's a bunch of machines, run by computer mostly."

"What's it tracking?"

"Something to do with weather patterns," he said. "They are testing the technology. Technicians go to the island and check on it every once in a while."

"So, like seismologists and the earthquake points, they monitor up and down the coast? They pull up the data, copy over the readings and then reset it?"

"Yeah, something like that."

"So, does it deal with earthquakes too?"

"I think they're probably taking readings of everything, but I don't really know," Nico answered. "They're mostly concerned about tsunamis, I believe, so earthquakes are likely a big part of it."

"Well, Japan would be interested in that, I suppose. Are tsunamis a big issue around here?"

"These islands are on the outside of Puget Sound, so they'd be the first ones to get hit, so maybe. But again, no people are there. Just equipment."

"So you say," Keane said. "What we really don't know is if that island for the top secret research is used secretly for something else or if some crazies are out there, killing people.

Really, logic doesn't always apply to every situation."

"True enough," Nico said cheerfully. "But you'll have as much assistance as you want."

"Well, for a job like this, we can hardly use a huge team. We'll draw way too much attention as we search those islands."

"Exactly. We do have the coast guard. They'll take you out to the area where these two women recently disappeared and show you where the other two disappeared earlier."

"Do we have a location for that distress call?"

"We do, and it's not the same exact location where these four people disappeared from," Nico said. "I'll send you all the data we have."

"So, we're not up against anything other than Mother Nature potentially or some psycho?"

"We don't know what we're up against," Nico said. "So don't make any assumptions that would close off any possibility."

"Great," Keane said under his breath. He looked at Lennox. "Sounds like we're heading out today on a cruiser."

"The coast guard will meet you in two hours and twenty minutes at the GPS location where the women went overboard," Nico added.

"So we've got transport to get there on time?"

Lennox tapped Keane's shoulder and pointed. Not too far off the wharf was one of the large coast guard cruisers. "So we're going on the *Acadia*?"

"Yep, you sure are," Nico said, with a laugh. "Gear's already on board for both of you. A Zodiac awaits you at the end of the wharf. The driver will find you."

"Meaning, we've already been tagged, and they're just waiting for me to get off this call?" Keane asked.

"You got it. I don't need to tell you that somebody's daughter is out there."

"Two somebody's daughters, right?"

"Yes. Two women. Plus, remember the husband and wife from a week ago who are now dead."

"And who were they?"

"Electronic reports are coming your way."

Keane stood and looked at the end of one of the docks and saw a Zodiac watercraft with a seaman sitting in the front and staring at him. "I see our ride," he said.

"I'll send you more information when you're on board." And, with that, Nico hung up.

Keane pocketed his phone and motioned Lennox toward the wharf and asked, "You ready for a swim?"

Lennox gave him a big beefy grin. "I was born ready for swimming," he said. "Why do you think I joined the navy?"

"Well, for this job, it sounds like we maybe should have gone into the coast guard," Keane joked.

"Same diff," Lennox said. "But a little bizarre."

"The whole thing is bizarre," Keane said, "and hardly a black-ops mission."

"Disappointed?"

"Kinda, yeah," Keane admitted. "I get that some of these jobs are pretty wild and wonderful, but I was hoping for a little bit more than the usual for me."

"Who knows what this one could be?" Lennox said. "Besides, I'm just backup anyway."

Keane snorted at that. "As backup, you'll be right in the middle of it," he said.

"Good," Lennox said. "I hate being bored."

SANDRINE COULTER OPENED her eyes enough to realize she was still in whatever cell they'd been tossed into. Nearby, her best friend, Brenda Leigh, was barely conscious, her eyes fluttering as she struggled with a head injury. Sandrine rolled over and crawled to the side of her friend. "Hang in there," she whispered.

"I don't feel so good," Brenda whispered. "What the hell happened?"

"Well, I know we left the boat," Sandrine said, with an attempt to crack a joke. "But I think you were swept overboard, and, when I saw you in the ocean, I jumped in after you."

She kept another suspicion in the back of her mind because she had no valid reason for contemplating the idea that they may have been pushed. Except that she'd received a nudge as she went over. But that would call into question the actions of the two men they'd been sailing with. "We were on the sailboat," she said to Brenda. "Remember?"

"Yeah. What happened to Greg and Scott? Are they here with us?" Brenda's breathing was low and shallow.

"I don't see them," Sandrine said. "Apparently somebody saved us, and we're in some shelter that's keeping us out of the weather," she compromised. She was very concerned that their reality was much worse, but Brenda didn't need to know that, at least not yet. "Just rest," she said. "You've got a head wound. It stopped bleeding, but you've probably got a concussion."

Brenda gave her a lopsided smile. "Always giving orders," she whispered.

"Well, if you'd listened to the one about tying yourself to the sailboat," Sandrine said, "you wouldn't have washed overboard."

"Or I would have washed overboard," she said, "and been drowned while towed by the sailboat."

"Not likely," Sandrine said. "I'd been keeping an eye on you pretty steadily." She hated to remember the horror when the catamaran had run into trouble in the storm and that Brenda was missing. Then Sandrine caught sight of her best friend in the ocean, crying out for help.

The guys had turned around the sailboat and thrown her a lifebuoy, but, when she couldn't grab it, Sandrine contemplated going into the water after her, when suddenly she was in the water anyway. She had replayed the scene in her head over and over. Had she imagined feeling a literal nudge, or had she jumped in instinctively to help her friend? Going after someone in the open ocean in the midst of a storm was a recipe for two deaths.

Unfortunately she had no clue what happened after struggling to stay afloat as the catamaran was tossed farther and farther away from them.

The women were now in a room, almost like a root cellar, with a dirt floor and made of rock on three sides, but the double doors in front of her were interesting. She'd tried everything, but they didn't open, and that's where her fear began. She refused to even contemplate being a prisoner.

The immediate problem was that Brenda's head wound hadn't been treated. They had no bandages, and the wound hadn't even been cleaned. Her hair should be clipped away and stitches put in. She wasn't lying on a clean bed and was instead on the dirt, where they had been tossed. Exactly the same position Sandrine had found herself when she'd woken up the first time. She glanced at her friend. "Any idea who brought us here?"

"No," Brenda whispered. "I just woke up here."

"Me too," Sandrine said. She got to her feet and walked to the doors for the umpteenth time. "There's a double door," she said, "but I can't open it."

"Somebody's got to open it from the other side," Brenda said. "Lots of big doors are like that."

"Which is a stupid system," Sandrine said caustically, looking around again. "I mean, if you're inside, how do you get out? Another door should be here too."

"There could be," Brenda said. "I'd get up, but, every time I lift my head, the pain is excruciating."

"Stay still," Sandrine said, moving beside her friend once more and dropping beside her. "Definitely don't move. I'll see if there's any way out of here."

"Don't forget to look up or down," Brenda muttered, just as her eyes fluttered closed again.

Sandrine sat back on her heels, wishing she at least had blankets to cover Brenda. Her friend would catch a chill lying on the ground like this. It was a warm July day, but, after being in the water, their clothing was still wet, and, with that head injury, Brenda wasn't likely to handle the additional stressors on her body that well. It was getting light enough now that, with any luck, Sandrine could do a full search. She had tried earlier, but it had been pitch-black. Not much had changed with the lighting right now, but enough sunlight came through the cracks around the doors that she could see better.

She walked to the wall and very carefully moved along, looking and feeling the surface until she came all the way around to the doors again. The problem was, it was all rock. Wherever they were, it was like a rock cave, almost like a ravine with some man-made roof on top. She could see beams closing it off, but the beams rested on the rock walls, so somebody had taken a natural formation and had adapted their needs to the existing rocks. It wasn't that the ceiling was superhigh either, but Sandrine had nothing to stand on.

When on her tiptoes, Sandrine could reach up and feel the wood, but she couldn't apply much pressure to lift up a beam. And the wood was covered on top. She didn't know if it was topped by a mossy or a grassy slope by now or whether more wood or even roofing tiles were purposely laid down.

She returned to the double set of doors that should have opened from the center outward and checked the pins on the sides. The doors were made of wood, not steel, but some crossbar must have been on the other side because she couldn't see any latch between the two of them but did see a shadow, and she wondered if a two-by-four blocked the doors from opening. Which would make it very hard for her to get out. She didn't have anything small enough to fit in the crack between the two doors, and yet strong enough to lift the beam on the other side. Somebody had put her and Brenda in here and had secured the doors deliberately.

She hesitated calling out but knew that her friend needed help, plus Sandrine didn't want to stay locked in here another minute. Taking a deep breath, she placed her mouth close to the crack between the two doors and called out, "Hello? Hello? Can you open this door, please? My friend needs help!"

She wasn't sure what to expect, but, when no answer came, she returned to her friend and sat down. Brenda was unconscious again, her breathing shallow and low. And, just when Sandrine thought all was lost, she heard footsteps. She raced to the door and waited.

# CHAPTER 3

As SANDRINE WATCHED and waited in the shadows, a bar was removed from outside the wooden doors, confirming her suspicion of a two-by-four closure. Then both doors were opened. She stared in shock at the soldier standing slightly above her. She hopped to her feet and ran toward him, climbing out of the enclosure. "Oh, my gosh," she said. "Thank you for opening the door."

Then she stopped because the look on his face was anything but nice. "My friend needs help," she said, motioning toward Brenda. "I think she's got a concussion."

"She'll be fine," he said. "I have food for you though."

She brightened at that. "Any chance of blankets?" she asked hopefully. "We need to be dry."

He shrugged. "What do you expect when you come in out of the ocean?"

"I was hoping for a way to the mainland," she said, not exactly sure what was going on, but whoever this person was, she doubted he was a soldier, regardless of his attire. At least not one from her country. "Is there any way to get us back?"

He shook his head. "Not right away. And I don't have any blankets with me."

At that, her hopes plummeted. "Do you have any spare blankets you can bring later? Or a way to build a fire? We can't have one in there. Not enough ventilation." She looked at the ground, fairly sandy with little bits of rocks. "We could build one just outside the doors though," she said. "That would help."

He shrugged. "As long as you don't leave this area, that's fine," he said, "but you'll have to forage for your own wood. And I don't want you gone for very long."

She hesitated, not sure exactly what was going on. "That's fine," she said. "Do you have any paper or matches?"

He laughed. "If you want a fire, build it yourself," he said. He turned and picked up a plastic container with a big flat lid. Giving it to her, he said, "This is your food." Then he turned and walked away. At least he didn't lock the door. But then she was at the base of a long rock face. The shelter that they were in had a lot more rock above it, and they were nestled in a little sandy cove.

"Wait," she called, running behind him.

He spun around and glared at her, his hand going to his hip.

That's when she saw his gun. She swallowed hard. "I get that no wood is here, that I can't build a fire and that you're not very willing to help us," she said, "but I do appreciate what you've done so far."

His hand dropped slightly, and he stared at her, assessing her out in the light. "Well, make sure you stay grateful," he said. "I don't have to do this." With that, he turned and left.

She took several deep, calming breaths, trying to figure out exactly what was going on. She wasn't sure if they were prisoners or whether his words were a veiled threat that more would happen to them if they didn't behave. But, as she looked around, only sheer rock walls and sand were here. She saw no wood, nothing to burn at all. Only more sand. At least out here it was dry and a lot warmer. If she could get

Brenda out here, it would help. Sandrine put down the plastic container and walked back inside, but Brenda was sound asleep. Sandrine frowned at that but took off her shoes and her socks, then laid them outside to dry. If nothing else they needed to get some of these wet layers off.

It took a bit to get Brenda's T-shirt and pants off. Sandrine wasn't even sure it was the right thing to do, but wearing soaking wet clothing wouldn't help her friend either. Sandrine laid them out in the sun as well, then quickly stripped off the outer layer of her own clothing as well. She was hoping the guard wouldn't come back any time soon, since two women in just their underwear might put ideas into his head that she didn't want there. She wrung everything out carefully and spread them on the hot sand, hoping they would take no time to dry. Then she went back in and checked on Brenda. Now on the floor without her clothing, Brenda was bound to be that much colder.

Brenda woke up at that point and stared at Sandrine. "We're still here?"

"Unfortunately, yes. I need you to come outside into the sunlight," she said. "I don't know when we'll have our visitor back, but I want us to get dry and warmed up while we can."

With a great deal of effort, Sandrine helped Brenda to her feet, and they stumbled slowly out into the sunlight. They had not even a rock to lie on. She helped her friend lie down again and said, "Try to get warmed up, okay?"

"The sun feels really good," Brenda whispered.

"I know," Sandrine said. "But listen. At least one man is here, so we can't stay in just our underwear."

Brenda opened her eyes and stared at Sandrine in shock for a moment. Then she whispered, "I hear you. Let's get as dry as we can."

That was the best she could do for the moment, so Sandrine headed to the plastic container and lifted the lid. Inside was a cooked fish and a few biscuits. She swallowed hard because the man gave her no water. And, while she didn't know what was down in the little corner where the rocks opened up to the ocean, it wouldn't offer fresh water. She realized she'd come up against another issue, and it wouldn't be an easy one to remedy. They would need fresh water far more than food.

Sandrine slowly replaced the lid on the container and returned to sit beside Brenda. If nothing else, Sandrine would sit and guard her friend while the two of them warmed up and their clothes dried off. Beyond that Sandrine didn't know what else she was supposed to do.

THE COAST GUARD had laid out the marine maps for them. Keane and Lennox were already at the initial spot where the women had gone missing. Keane had the transcripts of the coast guard interview with the two men, Scott and Greg, and had heard the guardsmen's search stories as well. "Any reason to believe the men deep-sixed the women?" Keane asked the captain in a low tone.

The captain looked at him and shrugged. "We've seen people do worse."

"I know it's pretty easy to get rid of somebody out here, particularly in ugly weather."

From where they sat, watching the currents, and from the patterns on the map Keane had, it was hard to say where the two women would have ended up. "I understand several islands are around here where the women could have landed."

"Yes," the coast guard officer said. "We've taken our boats around all of them and found no obvious sign of the two women washed up on shore or even caught up in the shallows."

"Okay. We'll take the Zodiac and hit each one of these islands as well," Keane said.

"The Zodiac is yours to use," the captain said. "We'll stay out here for the next twenty-four hours, unless we get called away before that," he said. "I'm not sure how much longer after that we can wait nearby. Regardless, we will return here as often as possible over the next week. Send a signal for a pickup, and we'll be there."

"Good enough," Keane said. "That's another potential issue. Maybe another boat picked them up."

"They could have been taken to all kinds of places, though nobody has contacted the authorities."

"That's the best hope we have," Keane said. "We can certainly hope for something like that."

But, in his heart of hearts, he didn't hold out much hope. He studied the map a little bit longer. "I think we're ready to head out."

"Good," the captain said. "Keep in touch. We'll expect a check-in from you every six hours. If not, we'll send in the cavalry."

Keane nodded and headed to the lower deck. Lennox waited for them with scuba gear, in case needed, but asked, "What else do we need in the Zodiac?"

Keane said, "Rescue and tactical gear." Unbeknownst to the captain, Keane also had his duffel bag with additional firepower, in case they came up against something unex-pected. Keane didn't like to be out in the middle of nowhere unarmed, plus the talk of that installation worried him. As did that distress call from a week earlier. The coast guard had no further light to shed on that phone call either, the officer said, but they had increased their search of the area, yet had never found anything to back it up in those initial days—until they found the couple dead thereafter.

With the gear secured in the Zodiac, Lennox hit the throttle, and he and Keane headed toward the first of many islands they needed to check, although one of the four largest were the estimated locations most likely to find the women. To start with, the men did a very slow pass around the first one, coming up along the shoreline as close as Lennox could, checking in the shallows and moving around each and every one.

As soon as they circled back to their beginning point on this island, Lennox put in at a small landing. It wasn't exactly a beach, but they could disembark and beach the Zodiac. Then the two of them crisscrossed the small island, looking for any sign of human inhabitants, but found no sign of anything, other than a few seagulls.

With the first island under their belt, they hopped back into the Zodiac and went on to the next one and did the same thing. They discounted the small islands first, and, when they came to the second largest, Lennox pulled onto a small beach with steep rock cliffs all around. After they landed and disembarked, pulling the Zodiac up onto the beach far enough that they wouldn't have to worry about it floating away with the tide, Keane and Lennox then stopped and searched the area.

"Interesting formations here," Keane murmured.

"I don't see any other way to search the top, except by air."

"And, if somebody is up there, how the hell did they get there?" he asked, studying what appeared to be really steep elevated sides to this island.

"I don't know," Lennox said, "but we have to check."

They had brought climbing gear with them and would need every bit of it, and they were both decent free-climbers too. They quickly scrambled their way up to the top and realized they only had to scale the first twenty or so feet, and then it was a much more gradual ascent. As they climbed, they widened the distance between them so they could keep an eye on the whole area around them. By the time they made it to the top, Keane noted a large plateau of a decent size. It made for a very unique island. They walked around at the top, searching along the perimeter, but found no signs of anybody.

"Looks like we're zero for three," Lennox said, "out of the four most likely islands."

"Unless they're dead or have been picked up by somebody else," Keane said.

Lennox just nodded. "I sure wish we had better intel."

"We have satellite images downloaded, but they don't show movement on any of these islands."

"Well, since we're here, let's take care of these little ones off to the right, and then we'll tackle the bigger one on our list," Lennox suggested.

"Good enough," Keane agreed. They were already well past midday and heading into early evening. "If we can get these little ones checked over today before sunset," he said, "I suggest we park for the night on the bigger island nearby."

"That makes sense. Otherwise, we can go back to the cruiser if need be."

Just then a crackle came on Keane's comm unit. He

tapped it to hear the captain saying they'd been pulled away to work a rescue mission. "We're fine," Keane responded, "at least for the moment. We've checked three islands of the four on our list, plus we've got four smaller ones to cover that we sighted nearby. Then we've got plans to park on the big one overnight."

"Good enough," the captain said. "Keep in touch, and we'll expect your next check-in at six hours from now."

"We'll let you know when we hit the big island."

With that, they boarded the Zodiac and kept working through their plan. The smaller islands were really small, but that didn't mean a body wasn't caught in the shallower waters between them. It was fairly slow and tedious work because they had to keep checking the ocean below as well, looking for anything out of the ordinary. It was almost dark when they finally made their way to the largest of the islands. They pulled the Zodiac up onto a small beach.

"What do you say we make camp right here?"

"I agree," Lennox said, and, hopping out, he stretched and rotated his shoulders. "You forget what looking over the edge of that boat does to the back of your neck and shoulders," he muttered.

"This island will take a whole lot longer to search too," Keane said, staring up at the various its layers. "It would be quite easy for somebody to get up the sides most anywhere here."

"We'll spend one day here, I imagine," Lennox said. "Look. It's almost dark. We may as well call it quits and start early in the morning."

"Sounds good."

The two of them built a small fire and laid out the bunk rolls they had brought with them. They didn't need much, since it was a summer day. Just to crash for a few hours so they could rest. Keane figured it would be daybreak by at least five, possibly four-thirty a.m. Once they had enough light to search the island, they'd be good to go.

Keane sat here under the stars, listening to the waves crashing on the beach around them. "It's pretty special out here," he said.

"It is," Lennox said. "But that's because we're both healthy, and our bellies are full, and we're not injured," he said. "Unlike these two women."

"And those first two people who disappeared, then were found dead. Out of all this, the damn distress call is worrisome."

"Right. That's a whole different story. Like you said earlier, we don't know of pirates in the area. So what gives?"

"Exactly. That's the part of this that makes me uneasy," Keane said. "The part that made me bring our duffel bag," he said, with half a smile.

"So far our search to date rules out any real chance for the women to be anywhere but this larger island—or another one of the other ones, farther out. And, of course, if this one's got decent camouflage, no way we'll find any research installation here."

"It's on this island though, isn't it?" Lennox asked, confirming.

"Yes, but, without the satellite imagery, I couldn't see anything. Could you?"

The two exchanged hard glances.

Keane shook his head. "I didn't," he said. "But that doesn't mean it's not here. How big is it anyway? Is it just something in the ground, tracking tremors, or is it something much worse, much bigger?"

"I did request that information," Keane said, "but Nico doesn't have any answers for us yet."

"Of course not. It's top secret need-to-know information that we obviously don't need to know," Lennox said, with a laugh.

"Well, is it a secret because they're killing people who have washed ashore or—?" Keane shook his head. "That's pretty far-fetched. It's not as if either of our two missing women washed ashore around here anyway. Their sailboat was quite a ways away, and they went overboard at least seven nautical miles from here."

"Way too far to allow for currents or even swimming to bring them here," Lennox said. "It doesn't make sense. Yet you and I both know that logic doesn't always enter these events."

"Agreed. So, if they were here, why would that be? How did they get here? And, of all places, why would somebody bring them here?"

"Unless someone was trying to help them but didn't want anybody to know because it would reveal where he is, maybe?"

"In which case we could be dealing not with an installation so much but maybe some loner."

"A prepper maybe?" Lennox asked, with a laugh.

"Out here?"

"Well, maybe not so much out here, but you never know, right? People choose places for their last stand all over the Earth."

"You'd think it would be more inland, where you could grow things and have animals for food," Keane said.

"Still, you have the ocean, which will give you pretty well everything you need anyway," Lennox replied sarcastically.

"Except for fresh water. The island sounds much dodgier either way," Keane said.

"True. I would think, if I went the prepper route, I would want to be on land. With fresh water around me, not the ocean. I would prefer lakes and streams, and lots of wilderness for the animals."

"Exactly. But a lot of crazy people are in the world, and a lot of people just want to be alone. This is a great place for people who want to be undisturbed."

"We're still guessing anyway." Lennox chuckled.

At that, Keane's phone buzzed. He checked it to see a text message from Nico.

**Any news?**

Quickly Keane tapped in a response. **Stopped for the night due to darkness. On the largest island, the last on our checklist for an immediate search. Nothing so far. Starting at first light.**

**Good enough**, Nico replied.

**Any further word on the distress call?**
**Nothing.**

"This whole thing is basically a waste of time," Lennox said, after Keane read the message out loud.

"It is, but, at the same time, although our mission is for a grim reason, it is nice to be out here again," he admitted. "After too many missions and too much training, you can kind of forget why you went into the navy in the first place."

"Because we love water? Because we love to be of service to our country? Because we're natural-born protectors?"

"Yeah, all that and more," he said. "Look at us. We're sitting here. We could easily be more sheltered backed up against the rocks, but we're down here close to the water, where I can watch the way the moonlight ripples across the waves. It looks like a storm is out there, and, if it crashes in on us, we'll be damned pissed off about it," Keane said with a laugh. "But, right now, this is pretty magical."

"I know," Lennox said. "I used to go camping with my dad all the time. We'd find a little island like this and just set up for the night. We'd stay, have breakfast and explore a little bit. Then we'd hop back into our boats and head to the next place."

"Most people, when they say *camping*, are really thinking *road trip*," Keane said with a chuckle.

"In our case it was boat trip," he said with a smile. "I was nearly born in a kayak for God's sake. They headed for land, and my mom gave birth to me, six weeks early," he said with a laugh. "They stayed for a couple days for her to recover and to adapt to having a newborn around. Then back in the kayaks they went and headed for home again."

"At least they went home," Keane said, laughing. "But that's very much the pioneer mind-set."

"Right. That was about all they had back then," he said with a smile.

"Well, we need to get some shut-eye so we can get an early start."

"I'll take the first watch," Lennox said.

Keane nodded, got up, taking his sleeping bag with him in case he got cold in the night, and walked farther up the shore to lay down in the warm sand. Using his bedroll for a pillow right now and crossing his arms over his abdomen, he closed his eyes. His last thought was that, if those two women were out here somewhere, he sure as hell hoped they were high and dry and a long way away from the latest storm threatening to break over the top of them.

Otherwise, their night would get much worse.

# CHAPTER 4

T HE THUNDER WOKE her first. Sandrine opened her eyes to a black sky and the crashing of thunder somewhere a long way away. But, as she heard a thunder crash the second time, she confirmed the storm was getting closer. She bolted to her feet, noting the air had chilled. Although she was currently warm, she could see it wouldn't stay that way. And it wouldn't stay dry either. She walked to her clothes and found her T-shirt and jeans were dry and quickly got dressed. She pulled on her socks and her shoes, even though they were sandy. Not knowing what the night would bring, she wanted to be ready. She quickly went to Brenda, and, reaching down, she gently woke her friend.

Groggy, Brenda looked up at her. "What happened?" she asked.

"We're outside. I need you to get dressed and warm again. Our clothes are dry," Sandrine said with a smile.

Her friend's words sounded fuzzy and indistinct. Some of Brenda's words made no sense.

Sandrine gently helped her friend and slowly pulled the T-shirt on over her head and then got her into her jeans. She put on Brenda's shoes and socks, like for a child. When she finished, Sandrine got Brenda up again and helped her into the little shelter they had. She left the doors open but propped Brenda up against one of the rock walls. "We have a little bit of food," she said, "but we don't have any water."

As soon as she said that, Brenda, her voice dry and hoarse, rasped out, "I need a drink."

"I haven't seen our mysterious guy again," she said. "At the moment we don't have anything to drink." And she hadn't gone looking for any water source either, and she kicked herself for it now. Though she didn't want to leave Brenda alone either.

Clearly a storm was coming—and fast. She wanted to bury her head and cry but tried to say calm. Opening the bin with the food, she put it all onto the lid, and set it inside the shelter. Just in case there would be rain here, she wanted to put the empty container outside to catch fresh water for them. As she stepped outside, it started to rain. She quickly stepped back inside and watched for a moment to see if any particular area was better where water might pool. The rain hit the rocks and ran off at one particular spot, so she quickly placed the container underneath, hoping to get at least a little bit for drinking water.

When it began raining in earnest, it came down in a heavy deluge. The only good news was the fact that she was gathering some water. She quickly moved the biscuits and fish onto a rock inside their shelter and put the lid outside as well. They would need all the water they could possibly get. She held it up off to the side, using it almost like a slope to run water into the big container. She was just far enough under the shelter that only her arm got wet. She stood here for a long moment, watching Mother Nature completely obscure the world around her. Behind her, she heard Brenda call out.

"It's so beautiful."

Sandrine looked over, but her friend was smiling, as if

staring at something completely different than what Sandrine saw. "Just lie down, Brenda. You need to sleep." Sandrine was worried.

Brenda turned her face, still smiling. "I'm so happy to be here," she said.

Sandrine stared at her friend, overwhelmed with fear. The two of them had been friends for over a decade now. Whoever would have thought they would end up in this scenario? Sandrine had to hold it together and do anything she could to help her friend. Right now water was their most pressing issue, and Mother Nature was very kindly assisting them with that. If they could eat and drink a little, it would help.

Then Sandrine had to find that guy and see if there was a way off the island. If he had a boat, maybe she could pay him, although she couldn't give him the money until she made it back home again. But she had money at home, and Brenda's whole family was wealthy. They would definitely get her home, if they could. Maybe this guy had a cell phone or a radio. There had to be some way to contact people. He had a plastic container for Christ's sake—that had to come from somewhere. He came from civilization, and, if he came from civilization once, then surely he had a way to get them back again.

Just sitting here and waiting for Brenda to recover or die was killing Sandrine.

She stared out at the rain as it poured and poured, and then, just like that, it slowed to a trickle. She stepped out and picked up the bin. Walking along the edges where the rocks were still dripping, she collected as much of it as she could. The container was half full by the time she was done, and that was huge.

Bending underneath one of the rocks, she took several drinks as it filled her mouth and then took a long drink from the container itself. Walking back inside, she gently held a corner of the container to Brenda's mouth and helped Brenda get a drink as well. After several long sips, Brenda smiled and said, "That's great coffee."

"I wish," Sandrine said. "But here is a bit of fish and some biscuits, so let's eat."

She carefully broke off some of the cooked fish and fed bits and pieces to her friend. Sandrine split the fish as fairly as she could, and, since there were two biscuits, they each had one. And then with the water Sandrine had collected, the women managed to get it all down. Although it wasn't the best meal in the world, it tasted fantastic because she was desperately in need of nourishment.

With some food in her stomach, Brenda laid back down, mumbling and talking to herself.

Sandrine reached out and, lacing fingers with her friend, just sat at her side. "Rest," she whispered. "Try to sleep if you can."

And finally, after a deeply troubling conversation with herself, Brenda curled up in a ball and went to sleep again. Sandrine had napped outside in the sun, and the last thing she felt like right now was sleeping. She wanted to explore but was worried about leaving Brenda behind. But reality won out.

She could sit here and watch her friend die, or she could try to get her some help. The head injury didn't look that bad on the outside, but she wasn't so sure about what was happening on the inside. Like swelling on the brain? The worst thing would be for Brenda to die and for Sandrine to find out afterward that some simple medical care could have fixed it. She partially closed the shelter doors so that Brenda couldn't be seen from the outside. Then Sandrine stepped out. The sand had absorbed all the rain, but only the top was wet, and everything underneath was dry. She headed down to where she could see the beach and stood there, staring out over the vast ocean.

The storm had left behind clouds that blanketed any sign of other landmarks other than just a great big churning ocean. All she could see was a small bay that wasn't more than fifteen yards across with white sand and the rough ocean crashing up on the beach and pulling back again. No way to know where the man had gone to. Sandrine's worst thought was that he had taken off in his boat and had left them behind. But she had no reason to think that somebody would be so cruel. Yet, at the same time, they had been locked inside what amounted to a cave. Why were they stuck in a small shelter like that?

Of course she wasn't still a prisoner, but, with no other way to get off the island, the stranger hadn't needed to put a two-by-four across the doors. They were stuck here anyway. Hating the sinking feeling that they were completely isolated on this island, she decided that, rather than stand here and worry about it, she would check and make sure she wasn't missing something else.

With the sky darkening, she headed to the far side of the beach, looking steadily out over the ocean and then back up to the rocky cliffs. She couldn't see any side valleys or ways to get out other than what appeared to be some stairs cut into the rock.

She walked all the way around this little beach, all forty-five feet of it, past the opening that led to the tiny bay where Brenda still lay, and then came back to the stairs. With the rocks and the waves cutting her off elsewhere, at least without a boat, these stairs were the only way out. And they went up. Taking a deep breath, she moved slowly and carefully as the stairs were wet and had no railings or any handholds. She got halfway up and looked down, then caught her breath and leaned against the rock wall.

"Don't look down. Don't look down," she mumbled to herself. She kept going up because it was really her only option, other than the sea.

She was terrified of going back down again. As soon as she came around a little bit of a corner, it widened and became a much shallower incline. At this point she was quite comfortable climbing, as rock was on both sides. As she came through by the cliff's edge yet up to the top of the island, she could see more trees and foliage and still more rock, but no houses, no signs of human habitation. She frowned as she walked around the surface.

*Where the hell were they? How had they arrived here? And who was the man who had brought them that bit of food?*

As far as she could see out over the ocean, absolutely nothing was out there. Nothing was nearby. They were caught on an uninhabited island. Stuck somewhere in the middle of nowhere, with water on all sides. For the first time she began to realize just how truly isolated they were. Not only isolated but alone. She walked around on the topmost edge as best she could, but nothing more was to be found, no matter where she stood.

Behind her were more hills, more rocks and more trees. She walked a little bit farther but didn't want to go too far because of Brenda and the encroaching darkness. Deciding that she'd searched enough for the moment, Sandrine headed back to the stairs. Going down step by step and hanging on to the rock face, she made her way again to the sandy shore and stood, looking at the ocean for another long moment, feeling the vast uncertainty of her future. Something was so incredibly awe-inspiring about nature, but it could also make you feel like a tiny insignificant speck in the whole scope of things. They were stranded here, and nobody seemed to give a damn that they were here. Not quite true, considering that the one man had brought them food and had let them out of their cave prison cell.

He must have wanted them to survive, so surely he'd be back again. She'd been so certain that he had to be somewhere on the island. But what if he had left, and now they were here all alone? Shaking her head, she returned to the shelter as the darkness settled all around her. Hopefully in the morning things would look better. But, for the moment, the situation looked pretty dire.

As she got to where Brenda lay curled in a fetal position, Sandrine propped open one of the double doors with a two-by-four, like they had a floor-to-ceiling window. They needed to stay warm tonight, but she didn't want to be completely closed inside either. She was grateful that she could dry their clothes and that they had managed to warm up in the sun, but now it would be them against the elements.

Although they were winning at the moment, Sandrine wasn't too sure she could count on that continuing. It wouldn't be an easy night. But, if she could get Brenda through it, there was a much better chance of her being better tomorrow. With that thought in mind, Sandrine wrapped her arms around her friend to keep her warm and closed her eyes.

HE WOKE TO a storm crashing overhead.

Keane hopped to his feet to see Lennox with the boat flipped over and up higher on the sand. "We need shelter," he called out.

Lennox called back, "I've got a small pod tent here."

They quickly snapped it out of its casing and inflated it really fast. With both of them underneath, they were out of the worst of the rain.

"Where did that storm come from?" Keane asked.

"No clue," Lennox replied, "but it sure came up fast. Hopefully it'll disappear that way too."

The rain itself wasn't a problem, but hypothermia was. They were both seasoned travelers and outdoorsmen, so they would be fine, but Keane couldn't help but think of the two women and how they were faring. The storm carried on for a good forty-five minutes. Absolutely no way could the women stand up to these conditions with no resources. If they were alive, that is.

Luckily the storm finally moved on, yet it was still dark. "Any idea what time it is?"

"No, but it's got to be at least four in the morning," Lennox said.

"Well, I was planning on getting up soon anyway."

"Right, but we won't be going anywhere, until this dries up a bit, and we can see."

"We may as well eat then," Keane said.

"If you want to get the food out," Lennox said, "I'll pack this up, so we'll be ready to start exploring at first light."

And that's what they did. Just a few minutes later they were eating protein bars, an orange, some beef jerky, and they each had a hot cup of coffee, using a small single-burner cooktop. Instant coffee, of course, but it was something. And they would take *something* in these circumstances any day.

With one last look at the storm moving across the ocean, Keane said, "I sure hope they managed to miss out on that."

"Let's hope they're not even aware that a storm passed through," Lennox replied. "It could be a shitty deal for them, depending on their circumstances."

"I think the worst thing would be floating out in the ocean and waiting for somebody to pick you up."

"Especially without training or supplies or equipment," Lennox said.

After breakfast, everything was quickly cleaned up and packed away. Next, they took a serious look at where to start.

Soon, with ropes, grapples and a small safety kit, the two of them headed out together. They didn't want to split up at this point in time because too many unknown factors were here. It would have been a normal search-and-rescue scenario but for that distress call a week earlier, followed by two dead bodies. That changed the game completely.

The cliffs rose all along the white beach. One spot had a more accessible cliff, where the climbing was a little bit less onerous, and, as they climbed higher and higher, they realized that the island had multiple levels. It would take forever to search. They started off splitting the island into quadrants and checked out the first quadrant, going as slowly and as carefully as they could. They had to consider the chance that somebody made it onto the beach and then climbed but maybe had gotten pinned or had fallen. From all angles they studied and searched the first quadrant and found nothing.

With that, they headed to the second quadrant, another

part of the beach where they landed but off to the east. That search took a little less time as parts of it were sheer cliffs, and no way anybody would come up or down on any of that. They also looked for any sign of the installation or an earthquake-tracking system.

Keane had seen one before, during a previous mission, but it had been buried in the ground. He was looking for any telltale flags or poles to mark it, but, so far, he had found nothing man-made. Just as they headed to the third quadrant, he stopped and pointed—indeed, one of the poles he had expected to see. They took a look and could see a US-government-issued tag on the top. He quickly took several photos and sent it off to Nico. **Is this part of the tracking system?**

The answer came back almost immediately. **Yes. Should be three of those.**

Good to go, so they kept on walking. That meant humans had been here at one point in time, but were there still? And who was recording this information? He sent their questions off to Nico, asking for a schedule of who would have come, when they would have been here last, when they were next expected to visit this island and what kind of data they were collecting. And, perhaps most important, was anything else on the island besides these three locations for the research installation itself?

With the one site tagged on his GPS, they moved forward to the back section of this third quarter. They followed a big dip in the plateau here. It rose higher on the right-hand side in the back quarter, but the island itself was at least one mile across, and so it was taking forever. He sent back a note to Nico. **We may not finish today.**

When Nico's answer came back as a text with a single

question mark, Keane responded. **Island huge. Heavy vegetation. Somebody shipwrecked could have made it into some of these spots and collapsed.** After a moment of silence, he sent another text. **A dog would help.**

He got a reply right away. **Want one airlifted in?**

He thought about it for a moment, then shook his head. **Everything's soaking wet, and, while a dog would certainly make it easier, we've already come this far, so—** He looked at Lennox. "What do you think about bringing in a dog?"

Lennox's eyebrows shot up. "You know what? That's not a bad idea." Yet, as he looked around, he said, "But everything is so wet, it would really play with the dog's olfactory system. Plus, we don't have any scent of the women for a dog to search for. It'll mostly be a case of search and rescue, looking for signs of life."

"Or signs of death," Keane said. "A lot of the dogs are quite capable of finding cadavers as well."

Lennox said, "Let's give it today, and, if we don't have any luck, then maybe tomorrow consider the search dog issue."

"Good enough." Keane passed that message off to Nico and kept moving.

"I don't see any footprints," Lennox noted. "I don't see much of anything up here."

"But that heavy rain would have washed so much away."

"Sadly, that's very true. And the cliff edges are almost completely impassable," Lennox nodded, looking around. "I don't remember this island."

Keane looked at his partner curiously. "Do you know this area?"

"Part of the family camping trips. But I don't remember

this island."

"Lots of them are fairly impassable," Keane said. They kept walking, searching, but found absolutely nothing. They heard only wind and saw the odd bird. As they stood on the edge of what they had deemed the third quadrant, he said, "It feels empty."

"I know," Lennox said, "but that doesn't mean it is." He lifted his hands, cupping them around his mouth, and screamed, "Hello." A massive gust of wind seemed to carry his voice forever.

Just when they were about to turn to head in another direction, Keane thought he heard something. He reached out, grabbed Lennox's shoulder. "Do that again."

Lennox looked at him, clearly surprised, but he willingly cupped his hands around his mouth and called again. And this time what they heard a response a little clearer. "Is that a person?"

The two men stared at each other and then quickly raced toward the sound. It wasn't easy to decipher, and neither was it easy to find. They found nothing on this level, so they worked their way toward a lower plateau area.

Keane saw a large grassy spot and was hoping for their sake that the women had made it that far. It took the guys a good hour to make it down to the spot, and, when they arrived, he had Lennox call out again. This time the response was clearer but had an edge to it.

As he came over the top of the grassy area and looked down, he spotted a hollow, where the ocean had carved out a deep, circular area, completely surrounded by sheer cliffs.

Down in the center a woman stood, and, as soon as she saw him, she screamed and waved her arms.

He called out, "We'll come down."

She nodded and called back, "We need help. My friend is injured."

"Radio the coast guard," Keane said to Lennox. "We should be able to get her out of here."

"I'm wondering if I shouldn't go back to the Zodiac," Lennox said, studying the lay of the land, as Keane brought out his ropes and grappling hooks.

"That's not a bad idea," Keane said. "Leave me the first aid kit, and, if you want, head back, grab the Zodiac and come around to this bay. I'll make my way down and take a closer look. Then we'll decide if the water exit is best and easiest."

With that decision made, he hooked up his ropes, and slowly, while Lennox stood at the top, Keane made his way down the sharp cliff face. When he was almost down, Lennox called out that he was leaving. Keane gave his partner a thumbs-up signal and watched as his friend disappeared from the top of the cliff. Down below, maybe thirty more feet, he could see the woman still standing there, waiting for him to land. "I'm coming," he said.

"Good," she said. "I was afraid we'd been deserted again."

He heard the word *again* but would clarify that with her later. And it was hardly the time to ask. Some of the rocks were coming loose as he descended. He stared up where he'd come from, and he could see rocks crumbling down over his head. As several bounced off his helmet, he swore, then ducked against the cliff wall.

She cried out and quickly ran, backing away from the rocks.

What was going on up there above him? Unless Lennox's movement caused rocks to shift, Keane wasn't too happy about it either.

Keane clung to the cliff and waited until the rocks stopped moving. When it finally appeared to be safer, he let himself swing back out and quickly descended. As he got down within the last ten or fifteen feet, he felt his rope jerking. He looked up to see his rope cut loose. He fell the last few feet, rolling clear of the rocks. As soon as he could, he picked himself up and raced back against the cliff's edge. He motioned for her to run toward him.

She stared at him in shock but quickly joined him underneath a little dip where the rocks could continue to fall without hitting them. But the rockslide stopped.

"Who the hell is on this island with you?" he asked in a harsh voice. His mind raced with possibilities.

She shook her head. "I don't know. I don't know," she whispered. "A man dropped off a container with a fish and a couple biscuits, but he wouldn't give us any blankets or towels, and he wouldn't help us get off the island. He just left us."

Keane stared at her, shocked at the turn of events, but no doubt she was telling the truth. She had her arms wrapped around her chest and held her shoulder, which even now oozed blood. He leaned over to check it.

"I got hit by some of the falling rocks," she said and reached up to touch her head.

He checked out both injuries. "At least they're superficial. What I need to know is whether we're facing one man or a dozen."

"I don't know," she said, her teeth starting to chatter.

He wrapped his arm around her and tucked her up close. "Look. I'm sorry. I don't mean to scare you," he said, "but my rope was cut." He pointed at the rope that now lay like a coiled snake on the sand amid the rocks beside him.

Her hand clapped over her mouth as she stared at it; and she just burrowed in closer.

He waited for a long moment and then said, "I need you to get ahold of yourself."

She nodded. "I know. I know," she said. "It's been two very long days."

"Start at the beginning, and tell me what happened," he said, as he studied the area around him. "Tell me what you've seen. Like, where did you see this man?"

"He—well, we were locked inside that little space up there," she said, pointing. "A two-by-four closes the doors. When I called for help, I heard footsteps, and somebody came and took the bar off, opening those doors. He brought us food, but he didn't give us any water, and then he left. He walked down to the opening there to the ocean."

"Did you hear a boat? Did you hear him leave at all?"

She shook her head. "I did see stairs going to a flatter spot up there, but I don't know where else he could have gone. And he hasn't come back. I looked all around at the top of this plateau, but I didn't find anything."

"Do you need water?" he asked, unclipping a bottle from his belt.

"We collected rainwater," she said, "but, yes, if you don't mind."

He quickly popped the top and gave it to her and watched as she drank thirstily. He waited until she was done and then sagged back in place.

"My friend is hurt," she said. "She's got a head injury, and she's delirious. I don't know what to do for her."

"Not a whole lot we can do except get her to medical help," he said, looking around. "I want to make it to where your friend is, but, if somebody is watching us, we don't want him to know that we're alive. Especially me."

"You're hoping he'll think you died in the fall?"

He nodded. "Yes, but I don't know how long it'll take for him to come down and check on me."

"Oh, God. I don't know," she said. "We can walk around this corner, but, at one point, it's exposed. And, if he's watching us, we can't stop him from seeing you."

"So we'll stand here for a moment and make sure he's gone," he said. "He could be on his way down, and, if that's the case, I'll have to find a way to capture him before he tries to hurt us again."

"If it wasn't for the cut rope," she said slowly, staring at him, "I wouldn't think that he was trying to hurt us at all. He did bring us food."

"I get that," he said. "Can you tell me what happened? Like, who you are, and why you're here? Let me start, I'm Keane Lytton and I'm here on behalf of the coast guard."

She smiled. "My name is Sandrine Coulter," she said, "and I was out sailing with my friends. My girlfriend, Brenda, is hurt. We were out in her boyfriend's catamaran. We've gone sailing with them several times before but never this long or this far away."

"And what happened? How did you end up in the water and wind up here?"

"Brenda fell overboard," Sandrine explained, her voice gritty. "We caught up to her in the water, and I threw her a lifebuoy, but she seemed unable to grab it, so I jumped into the water after her."

He raised his eyebrows and stared at her.

She nodded. "I know, not exactly the smartest thing to do. But I couldn't do any less."

# CHAPTER 5

"HONESTLY, WE'VE BEEN friends since forever, and I wouldn't let her drown."

"Understood," he said. "What about the men on the sailboat with you?"

"It's all a bit fuzzy," she admitted. "I was screaming for help and trying to get Brenda to the buoy, so at least she'd have something to hang on to. But it got sent off in another direction, and the waves crashed over us," she said. "I remember keeping the two of us afloat, but I completely lost track of where the catamaran went. I don't even know if the guys are alive."

"They are. They got the boat back safely and contacted the coast guard, saying that you two were missing."

"Oh, thank God," she said. "I was so worried about them."

"And you ended up here, washed up on the beach or what?"

"I think so," she said, "but honestly that is where it gets very blurry. Because I woke up inside that little sheltered area. The thing is, we woke up behind the doors, and they were closed, locked, so we couldn't get out. Now a really cold wind can pass through the island, and maybe the man thought that we'd be delirious and get hurt or something. I don't know. Because, once the man opened the doors and brought the food, he left the doors open."

"As if he wasn't too worried that you could go anywhere," he said sardonically.

"I hate to admit it, but the thought did cross my mind that he had no need to keep us locked up because we couldn't escape the island anyway."

"Which is possible," he said. "It is a fairly big island though, and I have searched three-fourths of it. Still don't know what's even here."

"It's not very easy to climb anyway," she said. "We've been sitting here, waiting for somebody to come, and nobody but that one man has."

"Well, I'm here now," he said, frowning as he studied her closely. "Brenda's father got me and my buddy in here to search all the islands. The coast guard hasn't given up, but, with the bad weather, they've gone off to rescue other people. They've searched the nearby islands from the coastlines and then walked the islands themselves and found nothing." He said, "We've searched seven islands nearby, before landing here."

"We've been here one night that I'm aware of," she said. "With the heavy rain, I managed to fill the food container he gave us with water, so we've been subsisting on that. But he hasn't come back."

"Well, I'd say he's back now," Keane said, pointing to the cut rope.

She nodded. "And that scares the crap out of me," she said, "because either he doesn't want us to be rescued or he doesn't know who you are and doesn't care, but he wanted you to join us down here."

"Or he was hoping I'd die on the way down," Keane said. "It wasn't exactly a friendly welcome."

"What about your friend?"

Keane's face turned grim. "Lennox is a hell of a fighter and a good man. I'll put my money on him that he makes it back to the boat."

"Boat?" She brightened at that.

"We have a Zodiac on the other side," he said.

She studied his face, then whispered, "Do you think it's safe to return to Brenda now? I don't like leaving her alone for long."

"She's probably better off alone over there than she is with us," he said, his voice harsh.

Sandrine winced at that. "How long before your friend gets here with the boat?"

At that, Keane's face narrowed. "I don't know," he said. "It depends. If it's a clean trip, he'll be at least two hours getting back to the boat. Another hour maybe coming around. If he's been injured or worse and can't get to the boat, it's a whole different story."

She stared at him in shock. "That sounds terrible."

"It's realistic," he said. "Either way, if he can get to us, Lennox will do it. He also has some communication gear with him, so he'll send out a message to the coast guard as soon as he can."

"Can messages get out from here?" she asked.

"Down here, not likely," Keane said. "But up top we should connect via satellite."

She breathed a deep and slow breath. "That all sounds so doable," she said. "I'm really, really glad that you're here."

He gave a clipped nod. "I am too. It sounds like you've been through the wringer already."

"You don't know the half of it," she said.

He looked at her curiously, as if she wasn't sure if she

should tell him something. He clearly read her face and gave her a hard look. "If you haven't told me everything, this would be a really good time to share. I need all the help I can get, figuring out what we're dealing with here."

"Look. I can't prove it," she said, "but, when I was screaming at Brenda to grab the lifebuoy, just before I went in, I'm almost sure I felt a push between my shoulder blades."

He stared at her, shocked for a moment. "Meaning, you didn't jump in after your friend? You were pushed?"

"I was planning on going in anyway," she said, "so I don't know if he made that decision for me or what. I just can't say. Such chaos was happening at the time."

"And which one of the men was it?"

"Scott," she said sadly. "My ex-boyfriend."

"And have the two of you had any problems lately?"

"We broke up a couple months ago," she said. "Before that, we had been fighting lots, and I found out he'd been with another woman, so I broke it off."

"And yet, you still went sailing with him?"

She winced. "It's a little hard to explain, but I had told Brenda about what happened. Except the part about me seeing him, she didn't believe it, and her partner swore that Scott hadn't been unfaithful. So the trip was a setup to try and get me back together with him."

"Without your permission?"

"Exactly," she said in a wry tone. "I admit I wasn't happy when I saw him there at the boat. They kept telling me that he hadn't cheated on me. But I saw Scott with that woman. I'd told him—and Brenda—that a friend of mine had seen him with her, had seen them going into our apartment in the middle of a workday, but it was me who saw them. I just didn't want to say it."

"Usually the truth works out better in these instances."

"There's no 'in these instances,'" she said. "How the hell does anybody know how to respond when something like that happens?"

"Good point," he said.

"It's not easy to deal with relationships. At least, not for me."

"No, it's not. And, in a case like this," he said, "there's absolutely no way to practice how you'll respond."

"Betrayal always sucks," she said.

"It does," he said, "but don't let it get you down."

"Well, if it wasn't for him, maybe we wouldn't be here."

"Do you think so?"

"I don't know," she said, "because, when you think about it, I wouldn't have been on that boat if I'd known he'd be there. And, if he hadn't been there, maybe we wouldn't have gone out quite so far. He's the one who urged us out into deeper waters. He wanted a *great sailing day*."

"So are you thinking that maybe he wanted this to happen? Maybe planned it?"

"No, I can't say that," she said, "but I don't know." She rubbed her face with both hands, confused. "Don't worry about what I'm saying. I'm sure it's just the trauma of everything getting to me."

"Maybe. Maybe not," he said. "We'll keep it in the back of our minds anyway."

"Yeah," she said. "I'm sure he would deny it all."

"Yes, I'm sure he would too, so it depends on whether anybody else knows or saw him."

"That would mean Greg. And I highly doubt he would say anything about Scott because they've been best buddies forever."

"So, for now, maybe we should just deal with the problems we have at hand. It seems like we have enough of those already."

"I agree," she said. "Not the least of which is that Brenda really needs medical attention."

He glanced around and said, "Well, I need to take a look at her first."

"Sure," she said. "I can walk over there, but I don't know how to get you there without being seen."

"I'll risk it," he said, "because it has to happen sometime." He walked up along the edge of the cliff and around to the corner. Then, at the last bit, he ran around until he was at the center of the double doors. He stepped inside and crouched beside Brenda.

Sandrine was at his side instantly. "She's been like this since I woke up. Sometimes sleeping, sometimes delirious."

"Give me the symptoms," he said.

She gave him the little bit she knew and said, "I don't know how badly hurt she is."

"That sounds like a concussion, but the injury itself doesn't look too bad. She may sleep this off and wake up feeling pretty decent."

"I hope so," she said, "because this really sucks."

"I know," he said. "Let's just stay positive."

"Well, I was feeling positive until somebody cut your damn rope," she said. "After that, I didn't feel very positive anymore."

"I have complete faith in Lennox," he said. "It would take a lot for somebody to take him down."

"Not really," she said. "Bullets would do that just fine."

He looked at her, his gaze narrowed. "Did you see a gun

on that man?"

She looked up at him in surprise. "Didn't I say so?"

"No, you didn't."

"Oh, crap," she said. "He's dressed like a soldier and had a handgun on his hip."

"Shit," he said. Pulling out his phone, he sent Lennox a message, but, as he looked at the rock walls all around him, he knew his call or text wouldn't go through. "I wish I had known that before," he said.

"Yeah," she said. "I do too. I'm sorry. What about your friend? Will that be a problem?"

"No," he said. "It is what it is. It would take an awful lot to knock Lennox off his feet permanently."

She swore softly. "So we'll just sit here and wait?"

"Have you tried to get around at the edge of the beach?"

"No," she said. "I tried to go both ways down the beach but was cut off by the waves and rocks. Then I climbed some oddly natural-looking stairs in the cliff, but I didn't want to go too far and to leave Brenda for too long."

"Good point," he said. "Are you okay to stay here while I explore?"

She sucked in her breath but quickly realized they really had no options. "Fine," she said, "but please come back."

"I will," he said. "I promise."

She winced at that and asked, "What if that guy comes back here?"

"You stay right here beside your friend. If he asks if you saw anybody, just say that I fell and then got up, holding my head and ran."

"Ran where?"

He looked around, then pointed at the ocean and said, "Right into the water."

"He won't believe me."

"Maybe not, but he'll head in that direction."

She shrugged and said, "If you think so."

"Well, if you come up with a better idea," he said with a laugh, "you go for it."

She shook her head. "Yeah, that won't be so easy. Please, just be careful."

He gave her a quick smile and said, "Stay here. I'll be right back."

KEANE TOOK OFF toward the beach. He had tried not to let her see it, but he was definitely worried about Lennox. Whoever that asshole was who cut Keane's rope had never intended for Keane to get back up onto the top ledge. Now Keane had other gear with him, but it still wouldn't be easy to get back up to where he was. That's why the rope was cut in the first place.

As he made his way along the rocky edge down to the small beach, he took a look around. From where he stood, he saw absolutely nothing but the gray wet and drying stone rock face. It was a bizarre little inlet here, but perfect for the two women to be safe. The fact that this guy had delivered food meant that he hadn't wanted to kill them. At least not yet. And he had released them from their little prison.

Keane had taken a good look at the lock on it too, and it would have been hard for a woman to get out of there. A strong man probably could break apart the wood and gotten out that way, but the women were already weak from their ordeal and were small to begin with. Plus, with one injured, the other one was unlikely to leave. Sandrine probably wasn't thinking about shattering a wooden door either.

He, on the other hand, could feel his temper rising, and it would explode if he found out anybody had hurt Lennox. They'd been good buddies for a long time, but this was a very strange scenario. Lennox also had the equipment to get a message out, and that message was imperative at present. Keane checked if his phone had service now that he'd moved, but he had no bars. He had equipment back at the Zodiac to set up offshore communication to the coast guard, but he had to get there first.

When coming on a trip like this, he had to minimize the amount of gear he would carry because every pound would impact how far he could go each day. As it was right now, Keane and Lennox had made the decision to leave almost everything with the Zodiac. But, if this asshole got there first, he could completely demolish everything they had and leave them stranded too.

That wasn't a big concern for Keane, as several people already knew where he was, and, if he didn't report in, the coast guard would send out another team. His immediate concern was flushing this guy out, taking him down and finding Lennox.

Keane stood at the edge of the rock, but the waves lapped up along the sheer sides, giving him no break to walk around. He didn't give a shit about getting wet, but if it was sheer rock all the way on the other side too, then returning to where the Zodiac was beached would be a whole different story. He also would have to strip down and leave whatever gear he had here. Also not a good idea. He found the stairs that Sandrine had mentioned, and, as he crept his way up, he found it interesting that the stairs were mostly naturally hewn. Maybe somebody had come along with an ax and had chipped off a bit more to make it a little more stable, but these were natural for the most part.

When he came to where it widened, he slid along the side and stepped out to where he could see the lower platform. And it was completely empty. Was this where the asshole had been when he had cut Keane's rope? As Keane headed to the side, he realized this part didn't drop over to the edge; it just came up against more rock.

He searched the area but found nothing that worried him. He kept on moving toward the Zodiac, hoping to find a way to traverse the uneven cliffside to get where he needed to go. His only other option was to backtrack down the stairs, then strip down and swim around to the Zodiac. The problem with that was a storm was out there right now, with the potential for another to pop up at any time during the day. The waves bashing up against the cliff were strong and would have no problem picking him up and tossing him against the rocks over and over again. He could handle a few blows, but, at some point in time, his body would wear down, and the damage would be too severe. He needed to find another way around if he could.

This guy obviously knew his way around the island, so it would just take a little more time. Keane tapped the comm device he kept in his ear but got no answer from Lennox. Keane didn't let himself get too worried about that because the harsh rocky conditions made technical communication difficult in the best of times. He kept walking through the trees all along the edge of the cliff, looking for another way down, sure there must be another pathway. Ten minutes later he almost missed it.

He thought he caught a flash of light as he walked past. Stopping, he slowly backtracked, looking carefully, and saw just a cut into the rock. He had to shift sideways in order to make his way through. The flash of light he'd seen was from a bit of shiny black rock at just the right angle to make a reflection.

He crept around the corner to see the island opened up and another small plateau rose before him. Surprised and delighted, he searched the area first, then made his way up on top and over to the edge. From there he could see a series of slopes that led down toward where the Zodiac was. What bothered him was that he saw no sign of Lennox. While still up top, Keane tried calling Lennox, texting him and using the comm radio, but got nothing in response. Keane frowned and made his way slowly and carefully down to the Zodiac, watching the storm out on the ocean, hoping it stayed away for a little bit longer.

When he got to the Zodiac, he swore. The tubes had been completely deflated. Cut with a knife so they could never be repaired. He was as stuck as the women were, and that was a game-changer. Pissed, Keane checked his gear under the pontoons. Expecting to find it gone, he realized that whoever had damaged the Zodiac hadn't seen the large bag underneath. He pulled it out and quickly set up the offshore communication and contacted the coast guard.

Unfortunately, he couldn't get through because of the static. He tried several different methods and still got no connection.

Finally, he sent a Morse code message, repeating it several times before hoisting the bag on his back like a backpack, looking around for any sign that Lennox had been here. But there were no new tracks. Which meant he hadn't made it this far. Keane backtracked the way they had gone up in order to see if he could trace his buddy. Keane headed up the original pathway they had taken, grunting with the extra weight on his back, but not daring to lose it. He also had a handgun pocketed close enough that he could access it if needed.

When he got to the cliff where his rope had been secured earlier, he was tired, worn out and knew that hours had passed. Sandrine had to be completely terrified that he hadn't returned yet. He stood at the top of the cliff and stared down.

He could see the little shelter and the door partially open. His grapple hook was still where he'd left it but with no rope attached because, of course, it had dropped to the bottom when it was cut. He picked up the grapple hook and hung on to it. From here he followed Lennox's tracks back. No sign of him so far. It took another twenty minutes before Keane found his friend, unconscious and lying under some brush. Keane quickly checked Lennox's wound to see a bullet hole high in his shoulder.

Swearing, Keane unpacked his first aid kit, and, keeping his handgun close by, he quickly patched up his buddy. Then he found a head wound. Now he had two seriously injured people, both on separate levels geographically on the island, both in danger of more trauma from being moved. And no way to get immediate help. He checked out the head wound the best he could and tried to wake up Lennox. "Hey, buddy. Can you wake up?"

Lennox murmured.

"More than that please. I need you awake."

Lennox opened his eyes and stared at him. Then they narrowed, and he whispered, "Please tell me that you got that bastard."

"Not only did I not get him," he said, "I haven't seen

him. He cut my rope when I was climbing down, and he must have taken you out shortly thereafter."

Lennox looked confused, but then it seemed as if the tumblers clicked into place, and he whispered, "You survived the drop?"

"Yeah. Once I realized somebody was up there, I scrambled down as fast as I could," he said. "I still fell about ten or twelve feet, but I'm fine. He dropped a bunch of rocks down after me too."

"Bastard."

"It's been hours since you left me though," he said. "I found the two women. One's got a head wound, and so do you, by the way," he said.

Lennox reached up and touched his head, then shrugged and said, "I can't really feel much. Always been a bit of a hard head when it comes to this stuff."

"Doesn't change the fact that you're injured and that we've got a wild card on the loose up here."

"We need to get help," Lennox said.

"That's not happening," Keane said. "He killed the Zodiac tubes."

"Jesus," he said. "What a pain in the ass. Now what?"

"I want to get you down where the women are," he said. "I've got the bag of gear we had stowed under the Zodiac. He didn't find that."

"Good," he said. "That at least has the blankets, a few emergency rations and the sat phone gear."

"Exactly. Can you stand up?"

Immediately Lennox tried to sit up, but he put his weight on his bad shoulder and collapsed back down again. "Son of a bitch," he said. "What's wrong with my shoulder?"

"He shot you," Keane said briefly. "Through and

through. In the fatty part of your shoulder."

"You mean, the muscle in my shoulder," Lennox corrected.

"Dude, whatever," he said with a grin. "Use your other arm and see if you can get back up again." Moments later, with Lennox standing, albeit a little shakily, Keane studied the rest of his friend and told him to take a couple steps.

He took several shaky steps and moved his legs around a bit, saying, "I could use some food and water, but I'm not doing too bad."

Keane handed him a protein bar and said, "We don't have much, so rations are definitely at a premium."

Lennox nodded and ate the bar slowly. "The shoulder's a bitch though," he said. "Everything here we'll need ropes for."

"Yeah, the shoulder'll hurt, but it doesn't look like the bullet did any real damage."

"So he hit me over the head and shot me?"

"I think he probably shot you, then came over and smacked you one for good measure. You went down, and he left you there. Or maybe he hit you from behind, then shot you and left, thinking he'd killed you."

"Seems a funny place to go down, with the bushes and all."

"He may have dragged you out of sight, so I couldn't find you," Keane said.

"Makes sense. So is this little asshole still here on the island, do you think?"

"I don't know," Keane said. "I haven't found him yet."

"Well, that seems like the first order of business."

"The first order of business is to get you down with the women," Keane said. "I can't keep running back and forth between two places."

"Right, but I'm not that badly injured," Lenox said, flexing his muscles and rotating his shoulder gently.

"Good," Keane said cheerfully. "Because you know I can't nursemaid you."

Lennox snorted. "The day I need a nursemaid—"

"I know. I know," he said. "Let's get you down to where the other two are."

It took twice as long, since they had to go a little slower to baby his shoulder and head and because they were constantly looking for whoever had shot him. "Do you even know if the women are still okay?"

"No. Not yet," Keane said. "I hope they are though."

"This guy thinks he's just gonna pick us off, right?"

"It's hard to say," he said. "When you think about it, the whole thing is just weird." Keane had to lead Lennox back around the long and slow way that he had found. It took several hours, and it was late by the time they finally made their way to the beach. He stopped, waited for Lennox to catch up and then pointed out the double doors that were opened.

Lennox shook his head. "Who the hell would even build that?"

"And why?" Keane replied. "I didn't get a chance to take much of a look inside. But we'll do that now."

"And how do you know she's even there?"

"The only way to know," he said, "is to walk over there and hope the asshole isn't waiting inside for us."

# CHAPTER 6

SANDRINE HEARD VOICES and peered through the wooden slats of the door to the cavern, not even sure why she was hiding. But, when Keane didn't return, she'd slowly grown more and more terrified. Instead of sounding worse, Brenda seemed to be sleeping much deeper, but she wasn't responding to any verbal suggestions or reacting to any physical stimuli. And that worried Sandrine too. She watched, looking for anybody to go with the voices. She wanted to rush out and exclaim they were saved, but, at the same time, she was damn afraid it would be another container of fish from that soldier guy, who had no intention of helping her and Brenda leave this island.

Worse than that was if he didn't come with more fish.

She didn't know where Keane and his buddy were, but she hoped they were still alive.

Her hands started to sweat as she sat curled up in an awkward position, leaning so she could see through a small hole near the bottom of one of the doors. As she stared out, she could finally see two men coming toward the shelter, one moving a little slower than the other. *Keane.*

He carried a large bag on his back, which is why she hadn't recognized him as the same man she had seen earlier. But he was talking to somebody beside him, so she assumed it was his friend.

She stood, relief washing over her. She stepped out and called to him. He looked over and raised a hand in greeting. She raced toward him, and, not even giving herself a chance to think, she threw herself into his arms. She blubbered as she cried out, "You didn't come back. I was so worried about you."

His arms wrapped around her and held her close. "I came back," he said. "I ran into a few problems, but I'm here."

Keane's voice was so reassuring and his body so strong and solid that he made her feel so much better yet again. She wiped her eyes, feeling hot tears burning in the corner of her eyes. "I'm sorry," she said. "I'm not usually this much of a wreck."

"Hey, don't worry about it," he said. "It's a stressful time right now." He motioned to his friend. "This is Lennox."

She smiled up at him, until she saw the blood on his head and on his shoulder. "Oh, God, did you fall?"

"No," he said. "I was hit from behind and shot—or vice versa. I'm not quite sure."

It took her a moment to understand what he meant. "Oh, my God. Oh, my God. Oh, my God," she cried out. "He tried to kill you?"

"Maybe," Lennox said. "He didn't stick around and finish the job, for which I'm mighty thankful."

Keane motioned for the three of them to move into the small shelter. "That rain will break again," he said, "and we'll get another deluge."

She looked up at the sky and nodded. "I'll catch more rainwater, if so."

"Have you seen the same man at all?"

She shook her head. "I haven't seen anybody," she cried

out. "Absolutely no one. That's why I'm so grateful to see you."

"Hey, I said I'd come back," he said gently.

She tossed him a wry look. "So you did. But I expected you back hours and hours ago."

He nodded. "I know. I had some trouble, and I had to find Lennox too."

"Where's the boat?" she asked as they reached the shelter. "When the storm clears, do you think we can get off of this island?" She hated the urgency in her voice and the anxiety. But, between Brenda and herself and now Lennox, she just wanted to get away.

"Well, we would if we could," Keane said, but his voice was grim.

She turned slowly to look at him. "What does that mean?"

"It means," he said, "that's possible but not immediately. Whoever attacked Lennox also slit the pontoons on the Zodiac."

All her hope slid away. "Seriously? He destroyed our way off this island?"

"Which means he has another way off," Lennox said. "We'll just have to find it."

She stared at him in shock. "We can't even get around the corner with the way the ocean's splashing up on the rocks. How will we possibly find any other way off here?"

"If one guy's here," Keane said, "then he has a way to get on and off. This is too inhospitable a place to stay long-term, unless he's got helicopter drop-offs or something else."

She nodded slowly. "That makes sense," she said. "But I don't understand what kind of a boat he could have that we wouldn't have noticed."

"He could have any kind," Keane said. "Look at how narrow your view is from here. You have the whole ocean out there, but you see just a sliver of it."

"Did you see anything when you were up above though?" she challenged him.

He grinned at her, loving her feistiness. "No, I haven't had time yet."

She paced the small space under the shelter. "But it'll get dark again," she said, "and we can't see anything until tomorrow."

"Which is why I'm leaving you with Lennox to help stand guard while I go up there to take another look around."

Immediately she protested. "What happens when you can't come back because somebody shoots you and hits you over the head?"

"Not going to happen again now that we're all aware of someone on the island who's unhappy with us," he said cheerfully. "And Lennox has weapons and comm devices. So, as soon as it's possible, he'll contact the coast guard, who is waiting to hear from us. And at 2000 hours, eight p.m. tonight, if they haven't heard from us, they'll set up a rescue."

She stared at him hopefully. "But they still can't come in while there's a storm, right?"

"Right," he said. "We were sent here for a purpose. To find you and Brenda. So somebody will come after us."

She let out a long, slow breath. "Well, thank God for that," she said. "So why do you even want to look for this guy then?"

"Because he's already attacked us, Lennox in particular," he said. "So I don't want him coming along and causing trouble for the coast guard either. The last thing we need is for a crew to come in, trying to rescue us, only to have this guy shooting them."

"No," she said faintly. "We don't want that at all." She dropped down beside her friend.

He squatted alongside her and asked, "How's she doing?"

"I don't know," she whispered. "She seems to be sleeping easier, yet it's deeper, like she's not even asleep, but—I don't know," she said brokenly. "If you nudge her and try to wake her, she doesn't do anything."

"Well, at the moment, she needs to sleep as much as possible," Lennox said. "I do have some thermal blankets in our bag. They're made for these emergency scenarios." He motioned at the pack on Keane's back. "Let's get that off and get some of this stuff set up."

Keane dropped the large duffel bag and straightened, rolling his shoulder blades back and forth.

"Is it heavy?" she asked.

He looked at her, and a smile kicked up the corners of his mouth. "See if you can lift it."

She frowned and walked over. She considered herself very fit, but she didn't know what weight was when it came to carrying it on her back. She thought forty pounds was a lot. As she tried to lift the duffel bag, she realized she couldn't even get the damn thing off the ground. She stared at him as Lennox bent to open it. Everything from food rations and water were in there, plus some electronic gear.

With great joy she accepted an emergency blanket, which she immediately wrapped her friend in. "This will make a huge difference for her," she said. "Thank you."

"You may want to make up a bit of a pillow with the

sand," Keane said, showing her how to do it.

With her friend hopefully much more comfortable, Sandrine returned and stared at the food. "Any chance of a little bit of food?" she asked hopefully.

"Absolutely," Keane said. Then he gave her a protein bar to start with and said, "When I get back, I'll go fishing too."

"I can set up something once I get this done," Lennox said.

"Okay, thanks," Keane said. "Just make sure you don't overdo it."

He laughed. "I've been fishing since I was a tadpole," he said. "I can do it in my sleep."

"Good enough," Keane said, then faced Sandrine. "I don't have much time before I lose the sunlight, so I'll leave," he said. "I want to check another quadrant of this island, and I'll need a couple hours, so it'll probably be dark when I get back. Okay?"

She bit her lip and stared at him. "I really don't like the idea of you leaving."

"I don't like the idea either," he said with a smile. "But I don't want to get ambushed or have somebody come in here with a machine gun and shoot us all dead."

She took a huge deep breath and slowly let it out. "I really didn't need that image in my head."

"Neither did I," he said. "So let me make sure it doesn't happen."

Unable to help herself, she gave him a hug and said, "Please hurry back."

"Will do," he said, as he stroked his thumb across her cheek and whispered, "Give Lennox some help if you can."

She nodded. "We'll be fine," she said, but she knew she was trying to reassure herself as much as him.

"Listen. Lennox has an extra gun, so, if a situation arose where you needed to look after yourself, make sure you use it."

"Right," she said. "We'll be fine. Go so you can get back again."

"Right. I'm gone." With that, he turned and walked down to the beach.

Lennox stared up at her from the ground.

She frowned at him. "Is it safe for him to go alone?"

"As safe as it is for any of us right now," he said. "Come on. Help me unpack some of this stuff and set up the comm unit. Then I'll go to the beach and set up a fishing line."

"You'll have to ensure that asshole's not watching us," she said. "That's how he chopped the rope that Keane was on." She pointed to the rope and watched as Lennox's face became a little more drawn and serious as he studied the coiled-up rope on the ground amid the rocks that had fallen.

"Keane is lucky to be alive," he muttered. "We can't have assholes like this running around."

"Exactly," she said. "It's been a pretty trying day. But some food would help."

"The bar not doing much for you?"

"No," she said. "It seems pretty sucky to complain when I'm healthy otherwise, but maybe because I'm healthy is why I'm also hungry," she said with a smile. She watched as Lennox sorted through the materials he had on hand and then asked him, "What will you use to catch fish?"

"You'd be surprised," he said. He had a small amount of wire that he cut and formed into hooks, then tied onto some line. He smiled and said, "I'll go try my luck. Otherwise, I'll set out a line on a stick and see if we can find a place to set it securely amid the rocks. Not to mention find something to use as bait." And he laughed obviously looking forward to the challenge.

"Good luck with that," she said. "I kinda want to come with you because I don't want to be left behind, but, at the same time, I don't want to leave my friend."

"Your friend is fine," he said. "Come with me if you want, but let's get going while the fish are moving. Once that storm comes in, they'll be gone."

She nodded and smiled. "Okay, I'm sold," she said. "Can I carry anything or help somehow?"

He bent down and picked up a stick off the ground. "Let's see if we can find more of these. I can tie a bunch together, but, if any decent-size fish are out there, I'll need something stronger for a fishing pole."

She nodded, and, as they hit the beach, she almost wanted to smile at the churning waves. It was too dangerous to leave now, even if they had the Zodiac. No way they'd get over these swells. Mother Nature was cranky right now; however, she was tossing them some long sticks. Sandrine walked out into the waves a little bit and grabbed several.

Lennox nodded and tied his line with the hooks onto the end of the bundle of sticks and cast it out into a small shoal on the right-hand side. "If anything's around, we should find something here."

She shook her head and said, "Never thought I'd be doing this today."

His grin was bright and cheerful as he flashed it in her direction. "We must be open to all opportunities in order to change the way we live," he said. "Sometimes change is good."

"Not today," she said darkly. "Not today."

KEANE KNEW HE didn't have much time before sunset fell, and he didn't want to go over the same ground, but he had to retrace his steps to a certain point in order to return to the first of the plateaus. Instead of circling around, he headed straight across to the trees on the far side. He hadn't mentioned anything to the others, but he thought he saw something in the back of the trees. It would make that plateau the most sensible location for the installation because it was the closest to the sea, yet still had a huge grassy area for camouflage.

With the descent of darkness coming soon, he had maybe an hour of fading daylight left. As soon as he hit the trees, he immediately melded into the shadows. He stopped and waited, listening for the sounds of anyone approaching. He'd crossed that pasture deliberately, hoping that someone would see him and would be forced to make a move. He couldn't understand why they would be here. Earthquake monitoring stations alone didn't wash. No way any of the monitoring was done manually.

No, this was something entirely different.

It could just be some guy was all alone and wanted to stay that way, but it was definitely odd. Sandrine had said he wore military fatigues, but she didn't know what kind, what country or whether they were real military uniforms or just some of the commercial-made gear often sold as army surplus. Everything was available online these days. Much to his disgust. He could get the plans for making bombs and all the components from various vendors without a problem. Huge online companies would deliver it to your front doorstep so you didn't even leave your house. Talk about enabling the psychos of the world.

When no sounds came from the trees around him, he crept a little bit farther into the expanse of trees—a band that appeared to be a couple hundred yards deep and a good one-quarter-mile long. He was right smack in the middle of it, and, in order to search it, he would check both sides, and that would be so easy. He kept walking right through until he hit the cliff face on the other side.

But, just when he thought he was at a dead-end, he saw another one of those tiny rock-face fissures. He walked through it to the other side to find another meadow plateau a little bit higher up as it climbed all the way through the fissure. As soon as he got outside again, he thought he heard a voice. Stepping behind the rock formation a little bit, he realized the voices were coming closer. Shit.

He quickly ran back to the trees and found himself a hiding spot off to the right and in the middle of the thickest of the bushes. There he sat and waited. From the sounds of those voices, two men headed toward him.

"The girls should be okay still," the one man said.

"You shouldn't have given them any food," the other one said, his voice harsh and caustic.

"Well, until we decide what we're doing with them," he said, "no need for them to suffer."

"A bullet would stop the suffering."

"We said, *no killing*," the first one snapped.

"What did you expect when you cut that rope?"

At that, the man groaned. "What the hell are they even doing here?"

"You know what they're doing. They're looking for the women. If we let them find the women, they'll take them and leave. Now you've made this a big incident."

"We're not even supposed to be here."

"And we aren't staying," he said. "It was just shitty timing."

"Well, what was I supposed to do? Just let them drown?"

"Hell, yes. Then we wouldn't be in the position of killing them now," the second man snapped. "Just because we were out in the boat at the time, you didn't have to point them out, and we didn't have to find them," he said. "We smashed up on the rocks ourselves. Our boat is useless now. You do realize that, don't you?"

"Yeah, but I did find them. We did bring them in, and we did save them. It would feel wrong to kill them now."

Keane's eyebrows shot up as he listened. He had his phone on Record, ensuring he had an accurate accounting of whatever was said.

"Killing is not in my nature. You knew that at the beginning. We didn't come here to kill people. We're supposed to just be scoping out the island to see if it would work or not."

"Well, the answer is yes. It would have worked, but now it won't because too many people know about it."

"We haven't done anything though," the first man protested. "We didn't get a chance to set up repeating stations or anything. Besides, who gives a crap about these islands? They are completely deserted."

"Sure, but, without a boat, you're stuck," he said. "I suggest we signal our ship and leave."

"And let them die?" the first man asked cautiously. "We could just as easily tie them up and take them back to the mainland and dump them somewhere."

"Like in the ocean," the second man argued. "If you think I'm letting them go once they've seen my face, you're dreaming. No way in hell."

"Well, they've already seen me," the first man said, "so I don't think it makes much difference."

"No," the second man said. "It means that you made the mistake. You're the one who picked them up. You're the one who let them see you, so you're the one who needs to pop them one."

"What about the guy you shot?" the first man said. "What about him? He won't live, you know."

"Maybe we should check to make sure he's still there," the other man said. "I didn't get off that good of a shot."

"We're just supposed to be checking out the system to see if we could pick up those satellites and bounce the signals as planned," the first guy said. "Just because we're trying to set up a communication system that will operate on the US satellites doesn't mean it's top secret or anything."

"But we don't exactly have permission to be here, and it's for our use, no one else's," the second man said. "The mission is compromised and at risk because we've been seen."

"But it's not worth killing someone," the first man said. "Just because they saw us shouldn't matter. Especially if we decide the island won't work anyway."

"It won't work now," the second man snapped. "Just remember. We took money for this contract, so we still need to find a place to set up a couple repeating stations."

"I don't get why it has to be out in the ocean," he said.

"It's for smugglers. Remember? It's not that hard to figure out."

"Maybe, but they've been doing fine without this communication system so far. What the hell difference does it make?"

"It's a warning system, they said. And I don't know if I believe that or not, but we were hired to set it up, and that's what we'll do."

"It's not our kind of gig," the first man protested. "Nobody said anything about killing."

"No, but they told us what would happen if anyone found out what we were doing."

"They didn't say we'd be killed," he said.

"No, but maybe I should have made sure it was spelled out a little more plainly for you," the second man said derisively. After that came an odd silence.

His voice turning snarly, the first guy said, "Don't you start in on me."

"Whatever," the second guy said, his tone off a little. "Let's go take care of those women."

"I still don't like it," the first guy said.

As they walked past Keane, he considered his options. The second guy would shoot the two women without a thought, whether his no-kill partner wanted to or not. But they didn't know Lennox was there with the women. Keane had no way to give Lennox any warning though. Keane was desperate to see what they had going on up in the back of this plateau and also where their ship was, but he couldn't let them fire on the women and Lennox.

Torn, Keane once again checked his phone and his comm system but got nothing. Just as he headed around to get in front of the gunmen, the two had stopped and stood there, arguing.

The first man raised his hands in frustration. "Look. We shouldn't leave all our stuff alone. I'll go talk to the woman," he said. "You go back and take care of the gear. I'd like to get on this ship and out of here overnight."

"Yeah, well, if you hadn't gone and cut up their Zodiac, we could have used that to get to our ship."

"I know," the first man said. "That was a bad decision. Much better if we had used it for ourselves and just left them here. We wouldn't have to kill them. They would have died on their own."

"Sure," the second guy said, laughing. "Perishing from lack of fresh water and food. That's a nice way to go."

"Whatever," he said. "Look. I'll go down, like I said. You head back."

"I'll head back, but I'll pack up first and make sure that the ship gets our signal."

"Right," the first man said, "but we should change our pickup spot to the new cove down where the women are."

"I don't think so. I don't want anything to go wrong with getting our ship in here."

"Well, they'll be pissed that we lost our boat as it is."

"Yeah, they will," the second guy said. "Just so you know, I'll blame you for that one too. We wouldn't have capsized if you hadn't been trying to pick up those women."

"Whatever," the first man said. "I told you that I couldn't just do nothing and watch them drown."

"Well, right now you don't have much choice," the second man said. "Go on, and I'll be down at the base soon enough. And take it easy. We can't afford any more accidents." And on that note, they parted.

Stuck, Keane decided to follow the second man, putting his trust in Lennox to handle the first man. These guys were watching and waiting for somebody to come their way. Keane didn't see a weapon on the first man, but he was probably the one Sandrine saw, and she had confirmed earlier that he was armed. Keane now knew the second one had been the guy who shot Lennox.

Clearly he was the more dangerous of the two, so it would be good if Keane could take him out. He waited until the second guy strode past, muttering all the while about imbeciles, fools and shitty-ass partners. After waiting a safe period of time, Keane crept up behind him through the same crevice walkway to see the guy with several boxes of supplies and his own gear.

He talked on a radio, signaling for the ship. "Change of location. Come in at the cove."

A voice crackled on the other end. "Storm coming in."

"Right. Come and get us first."

"Can't. Too much turbulence."

"We don't want to stay here overnight," the second man said.

"Can't come in. You can come out though. We'll come in as close as we can, and then we'll pick you up."

Dropping the microphone, the man swore. Now he had to tell the contact guy that they had lost their boat. Finally, as he sat here scratching his head, the radio crackled.

"Over and out."

"Boat isn't seaworthy."

Silence came first. Then *crackle, crackle, crackle.*

"I said the boat is no longer seaworthy. We can't get out to you. We need a pickup."

"Storm." *Crackle.* "No pickup."

The other guy swore and stomped around. "You fucking have to," he roared. "I don't want to stay out here another fucking night."

This time not even a crackle came from the radio.

Throwing the handset into the pile of gear, the second guy stormed around before stopping and glaring toward the ocean.

Following the direction of the man's gaze, Keane couldn't see any boat, but its location was obvious.

If his partner hadn't destroyed Keane's Zodiac, these two gunmen could have made their way out to their own ship and could have been picked up. If that ship couldn't get in due to the weather conditions, the coast guard probably couldn't come in close enough either. The coast guard cutters were something else, and they could run in the open sea in all kinds of weather. However, it would take a small boat to come to the island, so they could get on board and get back out again. And, with the waves coming in as strong as they were, Keane doubted anybody was going anywhere anytime soon.

Just then the guy spun around, as if he had felt Keane's gaze on him. Keane melted back a little bit farther into the rocks, desperately looking for a place to hide. He could climb up. A couple footholds and handholds were here, and a bit of a ledge was up above. Taking the chance that the scrambling noise he made as he climbed wouldn't be heard, he made his way up to the small ledge and stopped. The guy was halfway down the path with a handgun drawn as he searched his surroundings.

Keane stayed silent, studying what was in front of him. It looked like electronics and maybe a repeating station, with various parts and pieces. Some of that must have been airlifted in, since no way these two gunmen could have carried all that up the rock cliffs. But, as Keane studied it all again, much of it could be broken down, and, with four or five trips, these men could have done the delivery job easily enough.

Keane wondered if his own phone would work with that

station. He pulled out his phone and checked, but he wasn't getting any signal. He didn't have the other equipment with him either. He should have brought that too, damn it. Or maybe he could get access to the handset down below and contact the coast guard directly.

He knew the channel they were on. It was a marine radio, and that was the best thing for out here, an equal match to the one he had left with Lennox. If Keane could get his hands on that, it would help considerably. He hunkered lower and waited for the man to come closer. Best thing would be to take out this asshole and to remove him from the game completely. And, if Keane didn't kill him, the least Keane could do was knock him out and repay the favor for what he did to Lennox. And then the marine radio would be his.

He crouched and waited.

# CHAPTER 7

"WHAT DO I hear?" Sandrine murmured from the cave's doorway, her gaze scaling the rocks. "I thought I heard footsteps."

Lennox shook his head. "I'm not hearing anything. But an odd stillness is in the air."

"What does that mean?"

"It means that something is stirring."

She thought about that and realized what an oxymoron it was. How could *stirring* mean something was *still*? She shook her head, about to say something, when he grabbed her hand in warning. She saw somebody coming around the corner down at the bottom. "Is it Keane?"

"No," Lennox said in a harsh whisper. "Get behind that door."

"What about you?"

"He can't see me yet."

But Lennox did shuffle enough that the guy couldn't see him until he came up to the doors. "I'll move a little bit too."

"Unless he followed the footprints," she said, suddenly pointing to the line of them.

"But it's also the tracks that Keane made," he said. "And the two of us."

She nodded, then looked at the four fish sitting off to

the side of her now. "I really wish we could cook them."

"Once we deal with this guy, we will," he said.

"And what about Keane?" She'd been asking that same question for the last hour or more. It was almost dark. "This guy coming now is not bringing us food."

"And he does have a handgun," Lennox said smoothly.

She studied the man approaching. "It's the same man from before."

"Good," he said. "It would sure be nice if he was the only one."

"It seems doubtful," she said, "but I don't know."

As the guy walked up, he took a look at the rock cliff, saw the rope coiled at the bottom and frowned, looking around, probably hoping to see Keane's body.

"Now he knows somebody else is loose," she murmured.

"Yeah. Now the question he'll have is whether Keane is here or if he left already."

At that moment, the guy seemed to realize he could be in danger. He pulled his handgun from his holster and held it against his leg, but his footsteps were loud as he approached. "Hello," he said.

She poked her head around before Lennox could stop her. "Hello," she said. "Did you bring a boat this time?"

He shook his head. "No, I didn't.

"Food?"

He shook his head again.

"Oh," she whispered. "I was really hoping we could get out of here."

"Not tonight," the gunman said. "What happened to the guy who fell?"

She looked where the rope was and shrugged. "Did you see him fall?" she asked.

He shrugged. "I saw him fall, yeah."

"He got up, and he held his head and moved funny," she said. "He headed toward the water, and I haven't seen him since."

He looked at her, surprised, and looked at the rope. "Seriously?"

"Yeah, some rocks came down on him," she said. "He looked pretty woozy."

She could feel the stillness from Lennox beside her and didn't know why he didn't just pop this guy one. She quickly surmised that, in these tight quarters, as long as the stranger had a handgun, it would be too dangerous. Oh, for a sharpshooter up in the hills to take him out. She didn't even know if the gunman was responsible for any of this hell that she was going through, but this guy had obviously cut that rope which tossed Keane to the ground below.

"When are you getting off the island?" she asked.

"Our boat's damaged," he said. "So it'll be a while."

At the term *our*, she could feel Lennox stiffening, almost like a caged animal ready to blow beside her. "You mean, you're not alone?" she asked.

As if realizing the slip of his tongue, he shrugged and said, "No. I got a buddy here with me."

"How come he hasn't come down here?" she asked, curious.

"He's not feeling too good," the guy said.

Hesitantly, as if offering an olive branch, she said, "My name is Sandrine."

"Nice to meet you, Sandrine," he said with a hint of a smile. "I plucked you out of the ocean," he said. "You nearly drowned, you know."

She brightened. "Was that you?"

"Yes," he said. "It was me. What about your friend. How is she?"

She looked down at her feet and said, "She's not great. I can't wake her up anymore."

Immediately he frowned. "I'm sorry. That's got to be tough."

"Well, if you had a boat, I could get her off the island," she said hopefully.

"Not happening," he said. "At least not while the storm is going on. Maybe tomorrow."

"So, another night here? It's pretty damn unpleasant," she whispered. "Especially with no food or fire."

"I told you to light a fire," he said, returning to the caustic tone he had used earlier.

"Remember that part about no matches and no dry wood?" she reminded him, even though she knew that they had stacks of sticks inside now, something Lennox had insisted on.

"I got a few matches here," he said, "but I don't have any paper for you." He took a pack of matches from this pocket, and, walking closer, he tossed it to her.

She stepped out and caught them. "Well, I guess I'll take what I can get," she said, "but it won't help much."

He shrugged and said, "If you've got a guy hidden in there," he said, "you need to tell him to come out gently with his hands up."

She looked at him in surprise. "What guy?"

"The guy who fell when I chopped off the rope," he said, his tone turning mean. "I really won't take it kindly if I have to come in there and shoot him."

She gasped in fear. "You cut his rope to kill him, didn't you?"

"We don't like intruders," he said. "Sometimes you just have to bite the bullet and do the hard things."

"And what hard things are you talking about now?" she asked.

He lifted the handgun and said, "My buddy doesn't think you should stay alive."

She cried out and immediately stepped back. "Why would you do that?" she whispered. "Obviously you saved our lives. Why would you not do everything you could to keep us alive now?"

"He says you're a problem and that you need to be taken care of."

"I promise I won't be a problem," she said.

"You already are, apparently," he said heavily. "I'm sorry. I should have just let you drown in the first place." When he lifted the handgun, as if to shoot her, she gasped and dashed under cover again, and one shot rang out. He'd hit the wood beside her face. She cried out and whispered, "Please don't," she said. "Even if you leave us here, we'll still die. You don't have to shoot us."

"I told him that," the guy said, "but he didn't seem to like the idea."

"Doesn't matter what he says though, does it?" she asked. "Aren't you the boss?"

He laughed. "I'd like to think so, but I don't see myself keeping that title."

"But it is your deal here, isn't it?"

"Well, I'm the one who made the deal," he said, "but somehow my buddy has gotten a little bit more assertive than I expected. There wasn't supposed to be any killing."

"Well, if you're planning on shooting me," she said, "can't you at least explain why?"

"It's got to do with smuggling," he said, "but that's about all I can tell you."

"Shit," she whispered under her breath. Her eyes grew hard as she imagined just how much could be smuggled through this area. From drugs to sex trafficking. "This is a deserted island. It doesn't make any sense that this has got anything to do with us."

"It doesn't have anything to do with you," he said. "It's literally a case of you being in the wrong place at the wrong time. But then so are we," he said. "I wasn't exactly planning on having to kill you."

"Please don't," she whispered. "We've already survived a pretty horrific ordeal. Can't you at least just let nature take its course?"

"I wouldn't mind that," he said. "But my buddy—"

She heard him coming closer and closer. She grabbed a chunk of Lennox's hair. He nodded ever-so-slightly. "Please," she said, "I'm begging you. Don't do this."

"It won't do any good," he said. "If I don't kill you, my buddy will," he said. Another shot rang out. "Come on back out."

"So you can shoot me?" she cried out.

"Well, I'll shoot you whether you come out or not."

"Then you'll have to come get me," she said. "You'll have to come in here and shoot a woman who's already dying. And you'll have to shoot me."

"Nah, I won't shoot her," he said. "You're right. She is already dying."

"Then leave me with her," she cried out passionately. Even though she knew Lennox was here, it was just all too real of a possibility that this guy would come in and shoot her between the eyes. "You know there's no way for us to get off the island, so we'll be dead soon enough anyway."

She could feel him hesitate. "Please," she said. She peered through the cracks and watched as he lowered the gun.

He took a few steps back and said, "If he finds out I didn't kill you—"

"I promise I won't say anything to him. I'll stay inside and make sure he doesn't see us," she said.

"I don't know if that'll work though," he said. "He's pretty tricky."

"I really don't want to die this way," she said.

"Okay, but you're not allowed to sit there and blame me," he said.

"No," she said. "Of course not." But she wasn't exactly sure what she wasn't supposed to blame him for. Of course this was ridiculous. He had been trying to kill her, but he agreed to back away. "Thank you," she cried out.

"Whatever," he said. Just when she thought he was done, he stopped, then turned around and fired into the wooden doors.

She cried out and moaned. Then all of a sudden she went silent. She looked down at Lennox, who had one shot lined up. He took a slow and deep breath and popped off one shot. As she watched through the slats of the wooden doors, the gunman stood still for a long moment, then slowly fell to the ground. She glanced at Lennox and whispered, "Is he dead?"

"Yeah," he said. "He's dead."

She curled up in a ball and burst into tears. "Thank God," she whispered.

"It's okay," he said, "but we have to move the body."

"I know," she said. "I know, but I'm too damn tired."

"I got it," he said and hopped up and headed out with his handgun still at the ready.

When he got to the body, she realized that she couldn't let him move it on his own. Not with his shoulder injury. He'd likely start bleeding again. Quickly she raced behind him. A pool of blood was under the guy, and the bullet hole in his forehead was unmistakable. She gasped when she saw that half his head had blown away.

"Don't look," Lennox said, as he reached down with one hand and grabbed the guy by the back of the collar, lifting and dragging him toward the shelter.

"Why are we taking him here? Why not over in the corner and just bury him?"

He stopped, and a look of realization crossed his face. "I guess if we're here for a while, we don't want this guy getting smelly beside us."

"No," she said. "We don't."

Looking around, he found a little bit of a depression, a short distance from the shelter. He dragged the dead man over there, dropped him in and then kicked sand over him. Sandrine followed suit, and, using the lid from the container as a little shovel, before long they had a mound over him. Then she went back to the cavern's doors, and, using the same lid, she swept away the drag marks and footprints. She wiped away all the footprints back to the water, and then, with Lennox standing and watching her, she slowly returned to him. "I don't know where Keane is," she said, "but he needs to come back. It's getting very dark out."

"He will," Lennox said. "He will."

KEANE'S JUMP WAS clean, but the other guy had that sixth sense and looked up just as Keane landed on him. The guy roared as Keane's weight hit him on the top of his head and crushed him into the ground. There was no room to fight, and they were both on top of each other in a very narrow space. The guy tried to back up, but Keane got one hand free and pounded him in the face. The guy shook his head, backing up a little bit from the blow.

"Who the fuck are you?" he roared.

Keane tried to get another fist punch in, but there was no room. The other guy backed up a little bit more, trying to get his handgun up, but Keane got a sideways kick in, sending the gun flying harmlessly behind him. The guy swore, then turned and tried to race toward the gun. Keane followed and jumped him, sending the guy flying to his gut down in the pathway. There Keane pounded the stranger's face into the rock underfoot, once, twice, three times. After the third punch, the guy didn't move again. Keane quickly pocketed the handgun, then grabbed the guy by his arms and dragged him onto the narrow pathway where he had more light.

There he stopped and took a look at him. He checked for ID and found his name was Wilson. Keane didn't know the name. He laid everything out and took several photographs of it, then put it all back in the guy's wallet. Wilson had a hefty stack of cash with him too. Keane checked his other pockets and found a little notebook filled with names and phone numbers.

All good. Keane put that into his pocket too and then, dragging the guy farther inside, tied him up with rope he found with the guy's gear. Keane waited, hoping the guy would wake up, but Wilson wasn't showing any signs of stirring. Keane went through everything in his stash, finding a lot of gear that would send out a signal—similar to a lighthouse. But once it was triggered by a boat close by, it looked like it could probably turn on a light. He thought about it and shrugged. "Looks like a smuggler's deal."

"Not quite," the other guy murmured.

Wilson was awake. "So, what is it?"

"We were hired by them to set up a repeating station. They wanted to use it for signals. Sometimes, with the storms that come out here, it's really hard to find these rocks."

"Did you crash into them?"

The guy stayed silent for a bit. Finally, he asked, "Who are you?"

"Well, I'm not involved with smugglers," he said. "I came looking for the two women."

"Ah, shit. Those damn women," he said.

"Yeah, those damn women. People care about them. All you had to do was help them," Keane added, "and nobody would have given a shit about what you were doing here."

"Maybe so, but we couldn't take the chance. The people we accepted the contract from are not exactly friendly."

"Well, if you hadn't killed our Zodiac," he said, "I'd have been out of here with the women already."

"That idiot, Adam," he said. "he wasn't supposed to do that."

"You guys could have taken it yourself."

"Exactly. Like I said, he's an idiot."

The last thing Keane wanted to do was take this Wilson guy back to where the others were, but Keane couldn't take the chance of Wilson escaping and coming up behind them and causing trouble. Keane really wanted answers, but some of the answers would be found in their gear. He studied what was here and went through their personal stuff. "We'll pool resources."

He wasn't exactly sure what he should take with him, but Keane would need that bag of food supplies for sure. He quickly assembled what he could into one bag and left several other bags tucked under the rock face, in case he needed to come back for them. And then, walking over to his tied-up prisoner, he said, "Get up."

"I can't go anywhere if you keep me tied up," he said. "This island is treacherous."

"Well, you were planning on killing those poor women," Keane said. "Why should I give a shit if you live or die?"

The man closed his eyes. "This has been a shit deal from the beginning."

"Why'd you take it then?" Keane asked. He kept glancing toward where his group was, knowing that time was running out and that it would be even more treacherous in the dark. "Come on. We need to join the others."

"What others?" he asked. "My buddy already went ahead and shot them. You missed him."

"Well, my guy that you shot is down there with the women, and he's armed, so I wouldn't count on it," Keane said brutally. When he saw the look in the man's eyes, Keane nodded and said, "So right about now your buddy is probably dead."

His prisoner swore and closed his eyes. "Adam always was an idiot. He should have gone in quietly, seeing the lay of the land, and then shot the guy first."

"Yeah. Well, maybe he did. But Lennox isn't exactly a fool when it comes to this stuff."

"The problem is, we don't have our boat and can't get a

ride out until morning," Wilson whined.

"Neither can we," Keane said. "So let's get everybody down in one place," he said. "You won't fare so well out in the elements here overnight."

"It's just rain," his prisoner growled. "No predators are on this island. It's fucking uninhabitable."

"Oh, there's plenty of them," Keane said. "They're just all on two legs."

With that, the guy groaned and stood. His hands were tied in front of him. He looked at his feet and said, "Unless you're carrying me," he said, "no fucking way I can go up and down these paths." Looking at the bag Keane carried over his shoulder, Wilson asked, "And you're taking our fucking gear too?"

"Remember that part about pooling our resources to get through the night?" Keane said. "You've got food. Those women need it."

"It's not much," he said. "I know that idiot Adam already delivered biscuits and fish."

"One meal for two women every second day is not enough."

"It's never enough," he said, yawning. He sagged back onto the rocks. "Just leave me here."

"And then what?" Keane said. "You want me to come back for you while you're sitting in your own shit in the morning?"

The prisoner's eyes snapped wide open, and he glared at him.

"You didn't have to order the women to be shot either," Keane said, completely unsympathetic. "Now let's go." He kicked him again to the ground, facedown.

The guy snorted. "What do you expect me to do like

this?"

But Keane was already carefully working at his ankles. He changed the ropes, and, by the time he stepped back, got Wilson to stand again, the guy had two feet of slack in the rope between his legs, which would allow him to maneuver. "Now walk."

The guy looked at the ropes, surprised. "Not bad, but it won't help when it comes to climbing though those rock pathways," he said, "but I can at least walk a bit." He took several small steps, then said, "This will take us fucking forever."

"Well, I don't have forever," he said, "so I'll leave you to work your way down there on your own." And he walked past the guy.

As soon as he disappeared from sight, the guy called out, "Wait for me!"

"Hurry up then."

Keane waited in the darkness for the other man to catch up. Wilson moved really slow. Keane could adjust the rope and give him an extra six inches, but the more room he gave him, the more dangerous it was too. Keane turned and kept on walking the pathway. When they finally got to the other side, he walked out into the trees and stepped to the side, so that he could walk beside his prisoner. "What the hell are you guys even doing here?" he asked.

"Just setting up a repeating station," the guy said in a noncommittal voice.

But Keane had already heard an awful lot before. "For the smugglers?"

The guy just shrugged.

"That really doesn't make any sense."

"They're around here all the time," he said. "This band

of islands is well known on the maps, but they've still had several crashes. They just thought it would help if they had a repeating station here. Plus they'd have better telecommunications, and it would give them a way to track the islands."

"I'm surprised no lighthouses are out here."

"I know. Lots of islands in this area are treacherous," he said.

"You ever come on these islands?"

"No," he said. "Never. I'm not a boat guy. We ended up crashing our boat into the rocks when Adam saved those women."

Keane looked at him with interest. "Well, it was nice of you to save them."

"We should have let them drown anyway. We would have had our boat, gotten our work done and been gone. Instead we've got the goddamn women to deal with, no boat, and we have to wait for a pickup. Not to mention you asshats."

"Will the smugglers be pissed about the boat?"

"With our luck, they'll probably take our damn paychecks for it."

"That's a possibility too," Keane said with a nod. "Presumably it wasn't very big if it capsized with the extra women."

"Capsized trying to get the women in," he said. "I was on the back end with the motor, but it wasn't very stable. Once he got the one halfway in, and he tried to help the second one, it completely unseated us. When I went over to help—"

"A bad wave hit you broadside, and the whole thing went over."

"Exactly," he said. "And then all Adam would talk about

was saving them."

"Which was the right thing to do."

"But they became a problem, and, without that boat, we couldn't get off here."

"Unless you'd been smart enough to take our boat," Keane said.

"That wasn't me. That was Adam again."

"Are you sure Adam didn't have ulterior motives, keeping you guys on the island?"

His buddy looked at him in shock. "No. Why would he?"

"Well, why would you intentionally sabotage a Zodiac with a big powerful motor on the back end, knowing that you needed a boat to get off this island yourself?" Keane asked, studying the other man's face.

"I don't know why he did that," Wilson said reluctantly. "He gets into these weird moods where he thinks he's like some Rambo guy. And, if he got into some mind-set like that, he would have taken that knife he has and just plunged it into the hilt."

"Exactly what he did," Keane said. "It just doesn't make any sense, considering you guys were stuck on the island yourselves."

"Well, I don't know what the hell sense that guy makes," he said. "He's the one who made the deal for this whole thing anyway."

"So he just hired you to come along?"

"More or less. I'm the one who does installations like this one all over the place. But I've never done one on an island like this."

"So, it's all different for you."

"Absolutely. I can't say I'm terribly impressed either."

"And you did check on all the little details with your buddy?"

"I don't know what you're trying to say," he said.

"I'm just wondering if the deal really is the way you said it was. That's all."

"Of course it is. Why wouldn't it be?"

"Who the hell knows?" Keane said. "I'm just making conversation." But he was also making his prisoner think. He didn't know what Adam was up to with any of this deal. "Does your ship out there know that you guys need a lift?"

"Yes," he said.

"Interesting," he said, "and what did they tell you?"

"Basically that—I hope you're not suggesting that Adam wanted us to stay here overnight," Wilson said slowly.

"I don't know what I'm suggesting," he said. "It just made no sense to damage the Zodiac."

"I know," Wilson said, but his voice was thoughtful.

They crossed the meadow as soon as they came out of the trees and headed to the steep stairs. As they got there, he said, "Let's see if you can walk down the stairs at all."

Wilson took a few hesitant steps and then hopped down one, using the wall to help. Moving slowly, they made it to the last two stairs, where he slipped and fell. He swore as he landed on the hard rock and sand below. "I didn't need that," he said, shuffling himself into a sitting position.

Keane reached down, picked him up and helped him to stand. "Maybe not," he said, "but we're down here now." They continued until they came around the cove edge to see the wooden structure. He pointed at it and said, "Did you guys make that?"

He shook his head. "No, it was already here."

That response added to the disquiet in Keane's consciousness. "Are you sure Adam cut up the Zodiac?"

"No, but he did mention it." Wilson looked at Keane and glared. "I gave him shit for it, and he didn't deny it or anything." Keane just nodded. "Why? What are you suggesting?"

"Another party may be here," he said. "Why the hell would anybody put up this shelter?"

"Maybe somebody else was stranded here too," Wilson said.

"If Adam had said he hadn't done in the Zodiac, would you have believed him?"

"I didn't know it was punctured," he said, "until I came and saw it myself." He stared around, worry creasing his face. "Besides, if another group's here," he said, "that's bad news."

"True enough," Keane said. "That's one of the reasons I'm asking."

"I don't know who it would be."

"I'm afraid it could be some of your own guys," he said. "What are the chances you two have become redundant?"

"Hell no," he said. "That's not possible."

"Why not?" Keane asked.

"Well, they would have taken us out before now, if that was the case."

"Maybe. Or maybe not. Maybe they couldn't find you. Maybe they only found one of you."

"Do you think Adam's dead?" His voice had turned harsh. "If he is, it's probably you guys who killed him."

"Well, if he came shooting at my buddy or those women, Adam would be dead," Keane said.

"He didn't want to get rid of them, but, once he makes a decision, it's like a switch goes off in his head, and he heads into this other zone."

"And he's not really a soldier, is he?"

"No," he said. "He just likes all that gear. He's a wanna-be soldier."

"I was afraid of that."

"Why?" Wilson asked.

"Because those are the worst kind."

"Whatever," he said. "It's not like you're a fucking soldier. What do you care?"

"I *am* a soldier," he said. "Navy. And I do care."

"Again, whatever. Doesn't make a damn bit of difference. He'll be up there with everybody else."

Keane didn't argue the point, but he'd already seen the small mound off to the side, and, as far as he was concerned, a body was likely there. He kept Wilson moving forward at a steady pace, and, when they got nearer, Keane called out, "Hey! You guys there?"

When no answer came, he frowned and pulled the handgun from his pocket.

"What's the matter?" Wilson asked. "Don't you think your friends will be there?"

"No. I don't know that they are," he said, feeling his gut twist. He looked at his prisoner, who was grinning. "What did your friend plan to do?"

"He was just supposed to take them out," he said. "How he did that, I don't know. He does have a decent imagination though."

As they made it to the front of the enclosure, he looked inside at the gun at the ready to see that it was empty. "Shit." *Where were they?* Then he heard a hoot. Turning, he hooted back. Moments later he saw Lennox and Sandrine coming around the far side, where they had just entered via the beach.

Sandrine raced toward them and threw herself into his arms. He wrapped her up close, loving this sense of welcome. With her crushed tight against him, he looked at his prisoner, staring at the floor. Keane watched as the emergency blanket moved. Keane whispered, "How is she?"

"I'm not sure," Sandrine replied, quickly moving to check her friend. She pulled the blanket down a bit to see Brenda staring up at her. She smiled. "Brenda! How are you?"

"I feel like shit," she said, "and I'm so tired. It also feels like, if I move, I'll be sorry."

Sandrine chuckled. "That is true. Head injuries always make you feel that way."

"But I'm okay, aren't I?" Brenda asked, her voice weak and anxious.

"Now that you're awake and talking and looking a little more normal, I would say yes," she replied. "I, for one, am very grateful to see you back in the land of the living."

Brenda smiled and looked up. "Who are these men?"

"Well, these two," she said, pointing at Keane and Lennox, "came to rescue us."

At that, Brenda smiled and said, "Good timing for me to wake up."

"Very good timing," Sandrine replied joyfully. This was a wonderful reunion.

"Who is the other man?" Brenda studied the prisoner, her gaze frowning at his hands. "And why is he tied up?"

Sandrine looked at Keane and whispered, "Who is he?"

"He's your buddy's partner," he said. "He's also the one who shot Lennox." Keane turned to study Lennox, worried about the confrontation that he assumed had occurred in his absence. But Lennox appeared none the worse for wear and had a relaxed look on his face, as if he had not a care in the world. "What were you guys doing around the corner?"

"Seeking a change of pace," Lennox said with a smile.

Then he held up his hand, and Keane noted several fish were on the line. "Good, so we get to eat tonight."

"Only if we find something to burn for a fire," Sandrine said. "I'm not eating them raw."

"We've got some emergency fuel and a small campfire stove," he said, "so we can cook those. No problem."

With his prisoner off to the side, Keane dropped the huge bag from his back and said, "Besides, we have their supplies now too."

"Good," Lennox said with a hard glance at the new arrival. "So you're the asshole who shot me, huh?"

Wilson stared up at him. "Jesus Christ! How can you be alive after I shot you and clubbed you over the head?"

"Good to confirm it was you," Lennox growled. "I'll be happy to return the favor."

"What else was I supposed to do? I didn't have a clue who you were."

"You always shoot strangers?"

"These men were here to rescue us," Sandrine said, outraged.

"Well, we didn't know that," Wilson said, "and we didn't care. We didn't want anybody poking around here."

"Oh, I hear you," she snapped. "But your buddy tried to kill us."

At that, Wilson stopped and stared. Then he said, "*Tried?*"

She nodded slowly. "He tried. He didn't succeed."

And, just like that, Wilson seemed to cave in on himself. "Are you saying Adam's dead?"

"Yes," Lennox said calmly. "When people fire at me, I have this thing about firing back."

"That kid didn't know how to shoot anything," he said. "The gun was more for show and to make him feel proud."

"Maybe," Lennox said, "but those bullets were real."

Wilson winced. "I hear you there. He prided himself on that."

"Well, he won't anymore."

"God damn it," he said. "The kid wasn't yet thirty years old."

"We've also got another problem," Keane said. "We need to figure out if we're alone on the island."

"You mean, more than our two separate groups?" Lennox asked, narrowing his gaze. "Why would you think that?"

"I'm not convinced that Adam destroyed the Zodiac."

"Did he say he did?"

"Well, he said something about it, yes. But it doesn't seem logical that he would have done it, since they needed that boat to get off the island themselves. They apparently wrecked their boat when they picked up the girls. If they'd taken our Zodiac and left us behind, I would understand. That's logical. But to slash our boat so that it was no more valuable than the piece of junk they crashed on the rocks makes no sense, and I'm thinking maybe some third party sabotaged it, so Wilson and Adam couldn't leave the island either."

"So somebody came in and cut up the Zodiac and then left again, hoping that Wilson and Adam died right along with us?" Lennox looked from Keane to Wilson. "That's pretty cold."

"Well," Keane added, "I'm not sure our third-party knew about us per se. But he knew about Wilson and Adam for sure."

"Regardless, all of it is ridiculous," Sandrine cried out. She walked closer to Keane, her hand instinctively reaching out.

He was surprised to see his hand reaching back, as if a bond had formed between the two of them. Plus, every time he arrived, she came to him like a homing pigeon.

"Why would anybody sabotage a boat on an island?" Wilson asked.

"You tell us," Keane said in a mild tone of voice. "Why would somebody sabotage a boat?"

# CHAPTER 8

SANDRINE TURNED TO Keane and frowned. "You're saying it was deliberately damaged so nobody could use it?"

"So nobody could leave." Keane nodded.

She stared at him. "Then wouldn't it have been better if it was the guy we shot? Adam, was it? The guy who brought us the fish in the plastic container?"

Wilson nodded. "That was Adam. And that was our dinner that he gave you, by the way."

"Well, I appreciated that, and we both certainly needed it. But I sure didn't appreciate him coming back and shooting the place up tonight."

"Yeah, that'd be him too. He went nuts at times. He was normal most of the time. Then sometimes he would just go off half-cocked."

"Yes, I saw both sides of him. He was a little bit scary."

"It's also why he had trouble finding work and why some of his friends were a little bit off as well."

"And maybe he was also somebody the bosses could afford to get rid of," Keane said. "Maybe even a liability."

"I don't like your theories," Wilson said, "but it's possible."

"But you did contact your ship, and they said they couldn't come in tonight, right?"

"Yes, and I told them that we'd already crashed our boat."

"Were they pissed?"

"There was so much static that I couldn't really tell."

"Right," Keane said, nodding. "I wouldn't be at all surprised if somebody else didn't come in and take out the Zodiac, then checked out the lay of the land to find you. Chances are good that *that* someone is still here."

"And then will come back and pick them up?" she asked. "I want to be close by when that hap—" She stopped, surprised when Keane's arm tightened around her.

He whispered, "No, you don't."

She looked at him in outrage. "I do so. I want to go home."

"These men are smugglers, who you want nothing to do with," he said. "And, if they think that you'll interfere in their plans in any way or could tell tales afterward, they'll drop you where you stand. And, unfortunately for you, they're likely to use you hard before that happens."

She stared at him as all the color drained from her cheeks. "Jesus Christ," she whispered. "What kind of mess have we gotten into here?"

"Well, for that, you can blame Wilson and his buddy Adam. They rescued you from drowning at sea and brought you to this island, but I think it was a case of going from the fat into the fire," he said.

Her gaze went from one to the other, and then she shook her head. "Well, now you guys have to get us off this island, some way or another," she said, "because I refuse to be a toy tossed around between men, and I've already fought long and hard to keep Brenda with me," Sandrine snapped. "So it's up to you guys to keep us alive. You can get us off here somehow, can't you?" She studied Keane, and, when he smiled with just a twitch of his lips, she nodded and said, "Right. You've already got that organized, haven't you?"

He shrugged and said, "Well, maybe."

She smiled and reached up and kissed him on the cheek. "That better be a definite yes, not just a maybe." But, in her heart of hearts, she already knew that she'd picked the right side. And this guy would help her get her injured friend back home again. As long as nothing else went wrong.

Even knowing something else was going on or that he had some plans was enough to make Sandrine feel a little better. Then she wasn't so sure again as she stepped back into the little shelter and said, "I guess we just hunker down and wait for morning."

"To a certain extent," he said. "We'll spread out a little though. Otherwise, it'll get very close in here."

"Well, I'd rather be outside anyway," Wilson snapped.

Keane looked around, nodded and said, "That's not a bad idea." Then he helped him move outside of the double doors. Leaving the doors wide open for a breeze to come through, he looked at Sandrine and said, "I'll sit out here too."

She nodded but quickly chose to go where Brenda was. Sandrine sat beside her friend and whispered, "How are you doing?"

"Well, against all odds," her friend whispered back, "I'm still on the planet."

At that, Lennox chuckled. "And a good way to have it," he said. "Packing your body out of here would be a bitch."

Brenda gurgled with laughter. "I imagine it would be. Though I must confess that, while I'm grateful to be alive, I would much rather be in a five-star hotel, holding a glass of red wine, staring out over the city lights … from the bathtub."

"Ooh," Sandrine said, "if we're dreaming, I'll take that steak and prawns now." She kept up the light banter with her friend as she studied how fatigued she was. She asked Lennox, "I know we said we would cook, but is that anytime soon?"

Lennox nodded and got up, then closed one side of the shelter doors and started up his little burner.

"Did you close that for the wind?"

"Yes, and no," he said. "Partly so the wind won't blow out our gas flame and also so that we don't fill the cave with smoke." With his flashlight on, he sorted through the additional food Keane had collected from Adam and Wilson.

Outside it was silent, with neither of the two men sitting there saying a word.

Sandrine slid closer to Lennox. "Is Keane out there to stand watch?"

"More or less," Lennox said, his tone as low as hers.

"But, if anyone else is here, they can see him."

"Can they?" he asked, a half smirk on his face.

She thought about that, and as she went to peer around the door, he grabbed her arm and said, "Don't show your white face." From where she sat, she could barely see Keane. He blended into the rock so well. "That's amazing," she whispered.

"He's good at what he does," Lennox said.

"And you? Are you also good at what you do?"

"Sure," he said. "We both do the same thing."

"Is it safe to light a fire?"

"It's a calculated risk. We have this small burner for emergencies, but, in this case, a small fire will cook the fish quickly. I doubt you'd eat it raw." He looked at her questioningly.

Immediately she scrunched up her face and shook her head.

"Hence the fire," he said gently.

As he started cooking the fish, she realized they desperately needed this food right now. "There's such comfort in a hot meal, isn't there?"

"There is, indeed," he said. "We don't have a ton to go with this, but there are some canned goods."

"I'm surprised they brought cans. They're heavy and hard to pack."

"We have army rations. Not sure you'll like that any better."

"Any chance of a coffee or a cup of tea?" she asked hopefully. But the single burner was currently busy frying fish. He'd cut the fillets off the bone to make them cook faster and planned to cook one fish at a time in the small pan. While he cooked the first one, he was busy filleting the others.

She whispered, "Do you want me to hold the flashlight?"

"No, I've got just about enough light to do this," he said.

She brought over the lid and, with a little bit of water, rinsed off the top. "This is all I can offer as a plate," she whispered.

"It'll work," he said, and he quickly flipped the two pieces of fish that he had cooked onto the lid, then refilled the skillet with more. She couldn't resist breaking off a few flakes of fresh fish and tasted it. She moaned. "God, that is really good."

"Nothing like fresh food when you're hungry," he said

cheerfully. "Take that to share with Brenda."

Sandrine didn't need any urging and made her way to her friend. As soon as Brenda smelled the fish, she said, "Well, I guess I'd really like to try eating."

"Let's see if we can get you up on your feet or at least sitting up again," Lennox said, moving their way. With help, he and Sandrine got Brenda sitting up, then slowly and gently propped her up against the rock wall, so she could sit as the two women slowly ate the fish.

"I guess there won't be any more, will there?" Sandrine asked Lennox.

"We have some other rations, and there are quite a few fish," he said. "I was hoping to save some for breakfast, but I'm not sure we can."

"Will it keep overnight?" Brenda asked, sounding curious.

Lennox grimaced. "If we can keep it cooler—like, if I could put it back in the ocean—that will stop it from going bad overnight, but we'll likely eat it all now." He went through the motions and cooked another six fish. By the time everybody had one for themselves, a couple were still left. She watched as he and Keane split one, then handed one to the two women. Wilson protested outside that he wasn't getting seconds.

"You're alive," Keane said, laughing. "At least we gave you something to eat. That's a lot more than you let these women have." Keane stepped inside and rummaged around in the bags. "I think we still have some fruit leather, beef jerky and granola bars in here." He handed those out, while they filled the pot with water. As soon as the water boiled, he pulled out a disc, which then elongated into a large glass. He dropped a tea bag inside and poured boiling water over it for the women. Sandrine stared in fascination as a cup of tea was presented to her.

"I hope you don't need cream or sugar with this though," Lennox said. "I can offer you this much, but that's it."

"We'll take it," she said gratefully. With her arms wrapped around Brenda, the two of them huddled over the hot cup of tea, waiting until it was cool enough to drink. "This is absolutely wonderful," she whispered. "Thank you so much."

Lennox shrugged, then Keane handed over a pack of fruit leather and said, "You can also split a granola bar if you need it. If you don't need it," he said, "then save it, since we don't know how long we'll be here."

"I think we'll probably be fine," Brenda said. "My stomach is quite full after the fish."

"I could eat more," Sandrine said slowly. "But you're right, we probably shouldn't."

"See how you feel after the tea," Lennox said. "Having a hot liquid will help fill some holes."

She nodded, and, as Lennox sat here, Keane went back out and resettled in the rocks. She saw Wilson sitting there, staring up at the sky. While his arms were tied in front of him and so were his legs, he appeared to be quite comfortable. "What will we do about him?" she murmured to Lennox.

"Not sure yet," he said, glancing at the prisoner. "That's tomorrow's issue."

She nodded and smiled. The two women finished their tea, and Sandrine helped Brenda to lie back down again. Instead of joining her, Sandrine sat propped up, her head back, and just let her eyes close. When she heard a weird *zing* in her world, she opened her eyes to see Lennox standing right in front of her, a finger at his lips, whispering, "Do not move."

She opened her mouth, but he placed a finger against it and said, "We have company."

Instantly her stomach twisted and churned in fear. She nodded slowly. "Is Keane okay?" she asked, letting the words slide out on a breath.

He nodded. "They shot Wilson."

Her eyes widened in shock, but then, just like that, Lennox was gone. She laid down beside Brenda and wrapped her arms around her friend. When Brenda murmured something, she whispered against her ear, "We have to be quiet. Company's out there. Somebody just shot Wilson."

Brenda stiffened in her arms, and Sandrine kept whispering to her friend calmly and quietly. "The other two men are fine. They're on the hunt. Right now just the two of us are inside, and we must stay calm."

"Great," Brenda said. "Will we ever get out of this nightmare?"

HIDDEN BEHIND THE rock, Keane stayed motionless. The first thing he heard had been a tiny scrape up above. He hadn't expected to see any four-legged predators tonight. He hadn't seen signs of any wildlife, only birds. Which ruled out any other larger animal. The only ones at issue now were two-legged predators. He studied the cliffs around him. He had already memorized their natural shape, in case anything hunkered down and tried to blend in.

As his gaze went across once and then came back again

even slower, he stopped and studied one little hill that wasn't there before. This newest intruder had sunglasses on, hiding the whites of his eyes, and the glasses had a tint that would stop any reflection. But he was still taking a chance.

When Keane caught a reflection, he realized that they really did have a visitor. The shot, when it came, was both a surprise, yet not unexpected. What he hadn't expected was the target. Wilson's body jerked once. He'd been half dozing against the rocks and had never seen it coming. He never felt a thing. The only change was the blossoming red spot in the center of his forehead.

And that told Keane a whole lot more. It wasn't that easy to shoot downward, and whoever was up there was good at his job. But he wouldn't have come alone, and that meant at least one more guy was out there. Keane heard Lennox nearby as he whispered, "Bull's-eye."

Keane nodded and gave a thumbs-up. The figure up above quickly disappeared backward again. But was he gone? Did he suspect that his target was the only person here? Did he not care? Had he come and done his job, or had he not even realized that Wilson wasn't alone? With the first two gunmen now dead, the question was, who were these other men, what were they up to, and why would they have taken out Wilson?

When it was safe, Keane slipped toward Lennox and they both snuck silently to the wooden doors. "I figured two," he said, "and they likely came in where our Zodiac is."

"One going low. One going high," Lennox said, already strapping weapons onto a hip holster and securing a knife at his ankle. "Yeah, we'll need to take a little bit more weaponry with us though."

They headed back inside to the two women. Keane

caught sight of the whites of both of their eyes. "We're going after the shooter and his partner," he said.

Both women gasped but didn't say a word.

"Stay inside, and don't make a sound," Keane said. "We don't know that they even realize you're here, so let's keep it that way. They've shot Wilson dead, and they could be looking for his buddy Adam. In which case they won't find him, or maybe they'll just take off."

"What will you do?" Sandrine whispered.

"We're going after them. They got here somehow. That means they have some way to leave."

She nodded slowly. "Or they were dropped off."

"Or they were dropped off and somebody is circling the island. I haven't heard any boat motor though," he said. "Have you?"

"No, but it wouldn't take very much for them to cross that little distance in front of us during the storm, and we wouldn't have heard anything."

"Quite right," he said. He reached down and stuffed a granola bar and some fruit leather into his pocket and grabbed a bottle of water, then leaned over, gently stroked her cheek and said, "You'll be fine."

"Will I?" she asked, her voice low.

He smiled and said, "I'll come back for you."

She nodded gently. "Make sure you look after yourself," she said. "That shot came out of nowhere."

"Not quite," he said. "I did see the guy first."

She stared at him, awestruck, her gaze widening. "Magical powers or what?"

He smiled and whispered, "Remember? This is what we do."

She let out a long slow and somewhat shaky breath. "I'll

keep that in mind." As he got up to leave, she grabbed his hand and pulled him back down again.

Thinking she needed to say something, he crouched low and whispered, "What?"

Pushing herself up on one elbow, she gently brushed her lips against his. "For good luck."

He chuckled. "Then I better come back for good luck lots of times." Then he stepped out as Lennox looked at him with a raised eyebrow. Keane shrugged. "What can I say?" he said. "Women like magic."

"Right," Lennox said, shaking his head.

They shared a silent laugh, then quickly raced along the cliff. They were out of sight from anybody above but knew that the danger would be as they came around the cove. It would be interesting to see what they came up against. With the two of them moving silently on the rocks, Keane led them up the narrow staircase to where it opened up in the meadow. As they stopped and studied the area, Keane whispered, "Across there through the trees is another very narrow pathway," he said. "I found Wilson up on the top, and still more of their gear is up there."

"We may grab that too," Lennox replied.

"Later," Keane whispered with a nod, his gaze studying the trees, looking for movement or for any sign of something that didn't belong. But it all looked innocent, and, of course, that was the last thing it was. The better these men were, the harder it would be to find them.

Keane heard a noise off to the right and melted back against the rocks. Sure enough, he saw two men. Both of them carrying rifles. As they crouched down, they quickly dismantled the weapons and put them in their cases. In other words, they didn't think they had any further threats and were packing up, ready to leave. Keane watched silently as the two men moved efficiently and quietly.

They both had swarthy complexions, with darker skin, suggesting Latino backgrounds. They were good enough that he knew they had spent considerable time on the other end of a weapon. These won't be the same caliber of men as Wilson and Adam. These gunmen were ones who had been sent to clean up the mess.

Guns packed up, the two men stood and looked out at the ocean, one lifting his hand to study the horizon. "They're still not around."

"We're early," the other one said. "It was a little too easy."

"Yeah, but we only got one."

"They're always together," he said. "So we only got one. The other one isn't there to get."

The logic was interesting. Clear-cut and simple.

"Well, Mother Nature will take out the other one, if something didn't already. We didn't even need to bother in this instance. We could have just abandoned the two of them, and they would have been fine."

"Fine, as in *dead*, you mean." The man laughed. "How many times have we had to go in and clean up this shit? I'm getting tired of it."

"Tired in what way?"

Something in his tone had Keane melting farther into the shadows.

"You know what I mean," he said. "The money is good, but, after a while, you realize you've got to live in order to enjoy it. We spend all this time killing and accruing money, but we never get a chance to spend it."

"You know what happens if you quit," his partner said.

"Oh, I know," he said. "There's no quitting. That's just a fact of life in this industry. We were born into the smuggling world. It's not like we've ever had a chance to get out. At least we're in the independent world, not back on the mainland, following orders."

"Don't let anyone ever hear you say any of that though. I mean, I understand discontent," he said. "We deal with that all the time. But the thought about retiring? Yeah, you'll get a bullet between your own eyes if that gets out."

"I know," the other man said, but there was an edge and a wariness to it. "Don't you ever wonder about getting out in that ocean and sailing across to some completely different country and away from this lifestyle? Where you can sit back on a beach and see what that is like?"

"We haven't sat on a beach and enjoyed ourselves since we were kids," his partner growled. "And I don't have to tell you, Carlos, just how damn dangerous this talk is."

"I'm only saying it to you, for Christ's sake," Carlos said with a yawn. "Come on. Let's go."

"Well, you know what'll happen if you get overheard."

"I know," Carlos said.

"And what about the money? It's not like you'd do without that."

"We've got millions in the bank," he said. "If they had any idea how much money we had, you know we'd be forced to give that up too."

"I wasn't planning on telling them. It's our own money," he said. "It's our bank account."

"Oh, I get you," he said, "but we do have the money. If we wanted to leave, you know we could."

"Well, what you're saying is, we could in theory, but it's not gonna happen."

"Maybe not, but it should," he said. "One day it should."

"Well, I'm not ready yet," he said. "I want to keep living."

"Yeah, I hear you."

They headed to the far side, but not in the direction that Keane expected. He watched as the one guy stood again at the top of the cliff and said, "Still, it's kind of sad."

"What is?" asked the other man impatiently.

As Keane watched, one man turned to face the other, and a shot rang out.

One man stood, staring, clutching his chest. "Seriously?" Then he fell to his knees and smashed onto the ground.

The remaining man walked over, his rifle still pointed at his buddy. "Yeah, seriously. The money is in our joint account, for fuck's sake. You were either coming with me or I was going alone." He looked around at the options for the body and then swore, stripped it of gear and weaponry, and pushed it over the cliff's edge.

Keane and Lennox exchanged hard glances as they heard the sounds of the soft body hitting rocks all the way down.

"That's shitty," Lennox whispered.

But the last guy just stood there, his face up to the sky, almost as if he'd been freed from something. And then he slowly made his way to the far side and disappeared from sight.

The question Keane and Lennox had to answer was whether they would take out this guy or see if he disappeared quietly into the night? It appeared to be a falling out among thieves, but Keane and Lennox had learned long ago that there were times to get in a fight and times when it wasn't theirs to get into.

If this guy had a boat, that was a different story. But, in theory, Keane and his companions were probably getting picked up tomorrow. It was just hard to know how this would play out right now.

As the guy made his way to the far side, he stopped, looked back toward where Keane and Lennox stood in the shadows and said, "Shit."

Keane tensed, fearing the guy had seen them as he walked toward them. Keane looked at Lennox and shrugged as they both stepped out of the shadows and leveled their weapons at him. "Were you going somewhere?"

The man stopped in front of them, all anger and ugliness as he lifted his rifle.

Keane shook his head. "I wouldn't do that if I were you. Nobody'll spend your millions if you get yourself killed."

"Who are you, and what are you doing here?" the man raged.

"We came after the two women."

The surprise in the guy's face was shocking. "What women?"

Keane laughed. "The two guys who came here to set up your transmitting station rescued two women who had washed overboard. In the process, they crashed their own boat, and all four of them washed overboard."

"You're kidding?" He shook his head. "Those two were just a mess-up from the beginning. I couldn't believe it when the boss hired them. They said they needed a ride, but we were here to give them a bullet instead."

"Well, you took care of that nicely," Keane said.

"Not quite. I only took care of one. I'm one of those people who likes to cross my *T*s and dot my *I*s. I was heading back to make sure the other one wasn't hanging around anywhere."

"Don't worry about him," Keane said quietly. "We took him out."

"And why was that?"

"Because he was trying to kill the women."

The man's face was a confused mixture as he sorted through what he'd been told. "*Now* he wanted to kill the women after saving them?"

"Yes. The one you shot told him that he needed to."

"Got it. Well, he shouldn't have rescued them in the first place." He shrugged and said, "But we all have sisters and mothers and daughters. It's hard to watch women suffer."

"Unless you're into smuggling. Do you smuggle women?"

He shook his head. "No. Drugs."

"Of course," Keane said. "So now we're at a stalemate."

"What do you want to do?" the smuggler asked.

"What are you trying to do?" Keane asked.

"I wanted to ensure the other guy was dead and then take off."

"And your buddy? You'll just let the birds eat him?"

"The ocean will probably take him out to deeper water," Carlos said with a shrug. "I gave him a chance. You heard me practically begging him to come with me. I did give him a chance."

"Right. And now the question is, what chance are you looking for?"

"To return to my boat, to leave this island and to head off in the opposite direction from the bosses."

"Won't they come after you?"

"I doubt it," he said. "That's one of the reasons for setting the stage for both of us being dead."

"And you think they'll just disappear and come back in six months and see if anybody's still alive?"

"If I don't report in," the smuggler said steadily, "it won't matter, because they won't come looking anyway."

"Is that the kind of job you do?"

"It's the kind of job I've always done," he said, with a world-weariness. "Cleaning up messes. I'm just so damn tired of it all."

"And how can we believe that you'll just take off and disappear?"

"You don't need to," Carlos said. "But, if my bosses find me, I'm dead anyway, so either shoot me or give me a chance at having a decent life. I was born into this bullshit, and I've not had two seconds to myself to call my own, let alone refuse an order," he said.

"I'm not terribly interested in your sob story," Keane said, "but I want to make sure you're not bringing any other people back onto this island. We have enough trouble as it is."

Carlos laughed. "Believe me. Nobody's coming here after us. We're the last stop to clean up the bullshit," he said. "A ship is out there, but it's a good fifteen miles away. They won't come any closer. We either make it back, or we don't."

"What kind of boat do you have?"

"I have one down below," he said. "It's hidden."

"Are you the one who took out our Zodiac?"

The man looked at him in surprise. "Was that yours? Sorry. I thought it belonged to the other two. I was trying to make sure they didn't leave the island."

"That makes more sense," Keane said. "Yeah, it was ours. Speaking of which, another couple people were shot in this area a week or so ago."

He nodded. "Yeah, that was us. Like I said, there's no getting away from this work. They were in the wrong place at the wrong time. We captured them. I fought to keep them alive, but it wasn't going down well, so they were taken out." He shrugged. "It's a shitty life." He studied the look on Keane's face. "I can see you don't like my answer. But it's the truth. Why the hell do you think I want out?"

"Understandable but will you get out is the question?"

"If you give me a window, I'll take it. Chances are you have somebody coming in for a pickup then, don't you?"

"We do," he said. "In the morning."

"Let me leave then," he said. "No guarantee I'll make it anywhere with my boat as it is. It's small, and the waves are big, but it's my only chance at a new life."

"Good point," he said. "So disappear."

They dropped a line of fire at his feet, and he disappeared around the rocks.

"He didn't protest too much."

Keane exchanged a glance with Lennox, who just shrugged and said, "You know the ocean will get him, or his bosses will."

"I know. But he didn't kill any of us." Walking to the edge of the cliff, Keane looked down. It was too early yet to see Carlos, but, before long, he came through a little hollow, and there on the side, he tugged his boat into the water just around the corner. Another Zodiac type of watercraft, with black pontoons and a big-ass motor on the back. Keane wondered at the seaworthiness of it out in a big storm, but that wasn't his problem.

Carlos hopped in and pushed out until he could turn and pull at the engine. As soon as it fired up, he headed around the island, away from their view.

"Something tells me that's the opposite direction of the smugglers."

"If he's smart, it is, but he'll have to go up the coast to get away from this squall. He won't head across the ocean in that thing." But he let his thoughts trail off, because he didn't really give a shit. As long as they were alone now, he was fine with it.

"We need to make sure the other guy's dead and that neither left anything behind."

"He should have left enough behind so that anybody landing and checking up on them would see that they were gone."

"And what are we supposed to do? Add Wilson's body to the mix?"

"If we could ever get some comm set up," he said, "we could report what happened and let the coast guard or whoever deal with it."

They followed his footsteps, carefully navigating to the bottom.

"Are you getting the feeling that we should have killed him?"

"Not really," he said. "This has been a bizarre mission right from the beginning."

"I know," he said, "not exactly the same as the other Mavericks ops."

"No, but it's all good," Keane said quietly. "We're still doing what's right. We're helping others."

They checked to make sure that Carlos's partner was dead. His body washing up against the rocks along the shore wouldn't take long for nature to deal with him. Lennox and Keane left the body where it was and took several photos. They checked where the other boat had been hidden and couldn't see any signs of it left. If they hadn't seen Carlos leave themselves, they'd never have known he was here.

The two looked at each other, and Lennox said, "Let's head back."

"Yeah," Keane replied. "When we hit the top again, let's try to communicate with the coast guard."

"Good idea."

# CHAPTER 9

SANDRINE MUST HAVE dozed off because, as she woke up again, the sky around her was nowhere near as dark as it had been. As she lay quiet, Sandrine felt an almost rested and relaxed feeling, as if she'd gotten a couple hours of real sleep. She looked over to see her best friend resting peacefully. Sandrine's bladder was killing her though. She got up and shuffled outside, wincing at the sight of Wilson with the bullet hole still shining bright in his face.

"Poor guy," she whispered. With no place to hide to take care of her business, she headed off to the side, dug a small hole, quickly relieved herself and buried it. As she pulled her clothes back into position, she walked back to the cavern, remembering what Lennox had said about not being seen. But she hadn't even thought about it when she had bolted outside to go to the bathroom, and now such an odd sense to the air hung around her. She made her way slowly down to the cliff's edge and the water, wondering if the men were coming back or if something had happened to them up top.

And then she saw movement on the staircase around the corner. It was Lennox and Keane. She raced toward them, and Keane opened his arms.

"You should have stayed in the shelter," he said. "What if it wasn't us?"

She looked at Lennox, who was frowning at her. "I

know," she said. "I was supposed to remain inside and stay quiet, and then I fell asleep. When I woke up, I had to pee really badly. I didn't even think. I bolted outside, and then an eerie stillness took over. I knew I'd screwed up."

"Well, we found two other men," he said. "One killed the other and then took off in their boat."

"You didn't stop him?"

"It would have meant killing him," Keane said. "Something we don't do casually. He wasn't out to hurt us. It wasn't really worth taking him back if we could have kept him alive. Yes, he was an enforcer for a drug smuggling team. And, yes, I'm sure somebody gives a shit," he said, "but honestly that wasn't our priority just then."

"Neither was the boat obviously," she said with a smile.

"We have the coast guard coming to pick us up. Remember?"

She nodded. "I do remember, so that's good. What time is it anyway?"

"It's about four-forty," Lennox said.

She groaned. "So, not quite morning yet."

"Close enough, but we need to grab some shut-eye. It's likely to be a long day."

"Well, I can stand watch," she offered.

"You could," Keane said cheerfully. "At least you can with me. Lennox, you go down first. Your shoulder has got to be screaming."

He nodded, silently acknowledging Keane's observation, and they headed up toward the shelter. Lennox headed straight inside, and she watched as he dropped to his knees, laid down gently and rolled over onto his back.

"Just like that?"

"Just like that," Keane said with a smile. "We rest whenever we can, so we've learned to take advantage of the opportunities as we get them."

"Do you think we're safe now?"

"Well, we definitely still have some unknowns," he said, "but hopefully we are safe."

"And there won't be any trouble getting picked up, right?"

He smiled. "I doubt it." He motioned to the rocks where he had been sitting before, on the opposite side from where Wilson lay.

"Should we move him?" she asked worriedly.

He sighed. "We'll retrieve the bodies anyway," he said. "That'll be in the morning."

"You mean, in an hour or two," she said drily.

He smiled and nodded, then sat down, leaning against the rocks, and closed his eyes.

"Do you want to rest?" she asked. "I can certainly keep watch."

"I'm half awake right now," he said. "I do need to rest, but Lennox needs it more. We'll switch soon enough."

"Okay," she said and sat down beside him, a little bit of a distance between them, which she couldn't quite leave alone until she moved over closer.

He smiled when she snuggled up against him. "You're quite safe, you know?" he murmured.

"Maybe," she said, "but something about being alone for all those hours makes me appreciate the comfort of someone beside me."

"Being alone is both the best and the worst."

She thought about that and realized how very prophetic it was. "I've always loved alone time," she said, "but being alone with Brenda so very sick was just so devastating. I couldn't do anything. I didn't know what to do, and I didn't have the skills to deal with this outdoor living."

"Maybe not," he said, "but you've survived it really well." He rolled his head to the side so he could study her.

She smiled up at him. "What are you thinking?"

"Well, I was thinking about the push that sent you into the water."

She winced. "I keep trying to convince myself that I just imagined it."

"Any problems between the two of you?"

"No, I wouldn't have thought so," she said, "especially if he wanted to get back together. We were both up for the same job, so that caused a little bit of dissension," she said. "I got it, and he didn't. He ended up moving to a different location within the company—a different building actually. It made it less stressful to see him—or maybe for him to see me." She shrugged. "I thought it would be okay, but obviously it wasn't. He started to harass me when he saw me. On my way in and out from work. After we broke up, it was way worse."

"Surely that's not a reason to kill somebody though."

"No," she said. "I wouldn't like to think so … but maybe in a rash moment of anger or something. I don't know."

"Well, what I was told was that he had a garbled statement about how the one went in and then the second one went in. Both men said they weren't good swimmers, and, beyond throwing you guys life preservers, they were stuck trying to keep the boat upright."

She thought about that and then agreed. "I don't know if they are good swimmers or not," she said, "but I can imagine the waves would have been trying to send them into the water too. I'm glad they're both safe."

"Maybe," he said, "but did you think about what happens if he did try to kill you and if you make it back to
shore?"

She stared at him. "Well, he didn't come on shore and
try to kill me, so I'm sure he would write it all off as my
imagination."

Keane stayed quiet at that. "Tell me again about breaking up with him and how you got on the boat."

She frowned, not liking the way he was thinking.

"Come on."

"We were together for about a year when I found him
with someone else," she said. "So I broke up with him. I told
him that my friend had seen him with another woman, but
really it was me."

"Okay, and the boat?"

"I was supposed to go sailing with Brenda and Greg,
but, when I got there, I discovered Scott was there too."

"And yet, you still went out?"

"We were all friends once, and we still work together,"
she said. "I wasn't really happy about it, but Brenda did tell
me it had been Greg's idea and not hers."

"But Brenda still went along with it."

"I never told her that I was the one who found Scott in
bed with somebody else," she said calmly. "Scott and his new
girlfriend were so involved in having sex that they never
heard or saw me. So I ducked out of the apartment as fast as
I could. When he denied it, Brenda had hoped it was all a
mistake and that this outing might help. The whole job
thing made it more confusing too."

"But it was more than that, right?"

"Well, I found out about getting the job on the same day
I came home early to find him in bed with somebody else I

knew," she said. "I quietly left, then later told him that my friend had seen him with her in the middle of a workday and entering the apartment I shared with Scott, stopping to kiss each other outside on the front steps. It was a pretty ugly scenario. I moved out of the apartment, took a few things, leaving him all the furniture. I found a studio apartment closer to work, so I didn't have to commute. I thought it was all a done deal, so I was nursing my broken heart, working my new job, and I wasn't even thinking about him beyond the inevitable occasional contact at work. And then Brenda and Greg contacted me to go sailing, which is something we used to do a lot of. When I got there, I found out Scott was going with us."

"Wasn't that awkward?"

"Awkward, yes. But not as awkward as it would have been if he'd been there with his new girlfriend."

At that, Keane snorted and laughed. "Good point," he said. "So what happened? Were they really trying to get you guys back together again?"

"Yes, apparently. But the weather was building, and I was keeping quite a distance between us. When Brenda sat down beside me, she apologized, saying she didn't realize things were as bad as they were. I told her then about finding him in bed with this other woman. It was somebody she didn't know, but I had talked about her before, having seen that woman and Scott together at a coffee shop a couple times. I had believed him when he told me that she was an old friend. I'm very much the trusting type," she said drily.

"Again, both good and bad," he said.

She laughed. "Definitely. Anyway, it was a terribly awkward sailing trip. Then the weather got ugly, and things got even uglier when we ended up in the water."

"It sounds like it was also uglier because you're worried that he may have tried to kill you."

"I don't think he tried to kill me," she said. "More a case of getting angry for a moment and seeing an opportunity."

"Right. An opportunity to *kill* you," Keane said drily. "And didn't you tell me that he was the one encouraging the other guy to go farther and farther out to sea?"

"Yes, but—"

"No buts," he said firmly.

"Yeah, I guess. Fine. It is possible that he took an opportunity to take advantage of an accident. But it's not like he would get anything out of the deal, except the satisfaction of knowing I wouldn't be there to bug him again. I mean, I walked away, so he got the furniture and everything else in the apartment. So what the hell difference does it make?"

"Unless he wanted you back?"

"Well, that wouldn't happen and hardly makes sense to kill me then, does it?" she said. "I hold very few things in life really dear, but loyalty, honesty and honor are three of them."

"A woman after my own heart," he said. "That makes us dinosaurs in this world. You know that, right?"

"It's not the first time I've heard that," she said sadly. "My mom taught me these ethics. When she died of breast cancer a good eight or nine years ago now, that was one of the things I wanted to maintain for myself in her memory because she did the job of raising me right. The rest of the world is a messed-up place."

"Amen to that," he said, but his voice was getting a little slurred.

She whispered, "Just sleep. I'll keep watch. I promise."

He stirred. "I know you will," he said, "and I don't think

there's any immediate danger, but I'm on duty so—"

"Good, so just doze then. That internal radar system you have seems to work rather well."

"Oh, it does," he said. "It's just that, every once in a while, you can't necessarily trust it."

"I think trust for you is hard."

"What about you?" he asked. "You're the one dealing with the aftereffects of a cheating boyfriend."

"At least you said *cheating* and not *murderous*," she quipped.

"I was hoping you wouldn't defend him again," he said, his voice light.

She curled up tighter against Keane, letting her head drop onto his shoulder. When he lay his head to rest on hers, she smiled and just held his arm close. Something was very soothing about being out here. She could see the whitecaps bouncing off the waves in the distance—only a couple hundred yards away—but they were protected in this alcove. That was a very strange thing to say, considering the fact that a sharpshooter had taken out Wilson. She stared at the dead man, feeling a sense of peace and unease at the same time. She was amazed at the human ability to cope under stress and to make the abnormal normal in order to deal with it.

She'd never seen a dead man before; yet here she was already dealing with Adam and Wilson. She'd never been almost drowned or had to deal with her best friend being critically injured out in the middle of nowhere like Brenda had been, but it was yet another sign of how Sandrine was coping. Maybe her connection, this bond she felt toward Keane, was the same thing, but she hoped not. She didn't want it to be a stress response or a coping mechanism.

Something was so very special about him. He was so

different from her last boyfriend, and that was a bonus in itself.

She had been the one who had told Keane about the push in the middle of her shoulder blades, and, as she lay here with her eyes closed, she relived that moment when she was panicked because Brenda was in the water. Sandrine threw that life preserver at her, seeing Brenda struggling to keep her head abovewater. Sandrine had just made the decision that she should go in after her when she felt that hand—a solid thumb, long fingers and a palm pressed up against her back—and it pushed. It wasn't a case of *Hold on. Don't jump* or *Careful or you'll fall in.* No, it was clearly a shove, and she realized that her ex-boyfriend really had tried to kill her.

As she lay here dry-eyed in the morning light, she had to wonder, *What would she do about it?*

She was pondering her options when Lennox came out of the shelter. He looked at Keane and quietly said, "Your turn to crash."

As awake as ever, Keane replied softly, "Okay." He looked down at Sandrine at his side and whispered, "I'll go crash. Are you okay here, or do you want to come with me?"

She grinned. "I'm coming with you." She slowly stood, groaning as her body unwound itself from her very uncomfortable position up against the rocks. She followed him into the shelter, checking on Brenda first, relieved that she slept normally. "Looks like Brenda'll be okay," she said, as she settled in the sand beside Keane.

He rolled over, wrapped himself around her, and she snuggled back, spoon style, and closed her eyes. She could feel his chest rise and fall in a deep rhythm behind her. It amazed her that he was so capable of dropping off like that.

A skill she should try to cultivate, so she yawned once, closed her eyes and fell asleep.

KEANE SLIPPED FROM the cozy position with Sandrine wrapped in his arms and stepped outside to relieve himself. He then walked to where Lennox sat near the water, pulling in a fish. "You're really good at that," he said.

"Practice," Lennox replied. "It might not be the ideal food, but it's good and fresh, at least."

"Any thoughts on the smuggler?" Keane asked.

Lennox shook his head. "No. I think Mother Nature will take care of him. At least I hope so."

"We need to contact the coast guard."

"I already did," Lennox said. "They're on their way. Apparently the two boyfriends are with them."

"What? Why?"

"They were trying to show everybody exactly where the women had gone missing because apparently they didn't trust that the coast guard would find them."

"We gave them coordinates."

"I guess the admiral, Brenda's father, approved it."

"Of course he did. Something you need to know," he said quietly. Then he told Lennox what Sandrine had said about her ex-boyfriend pushing her into the ocean.

Lennox sat back and stared at him. "Seriously?"

"She hinted at it earlier, unsure that she wasn't just overly upset. But I quizzed her about it, while you were sleeping. I don't like it. We'll talk to her more this morning, and we probably should talk to Brenda as well," he said.

"Wow, so we have a murderer on board?"

"Attempted murderer anyway," Keane said. "And I'm wondering if that isn't partly why he's trying to get onto the coast guard ship."

"Uh-oh," Lennox said.

"Right, so he can finish the job."

Lennox studied him to see if he was serious and then shook his head. "It's a pitiful world out there. But, if he does finish the job, he doesn't have to face her accusations that he tried to kill her, does he?"

"Nope. She has no proof either."

"And, given the circumstances and what she's been through, it would be easy to suggest she made it up."

"Particularly if he can use the breakup—or, hell, the fact she got the big promotion and he didn't—and say she's just after revenge."

"And he gets away with it," Lennox said.

"Exactly," he said. "Something I'm not a big fan of."

"And yet, you are a big fan of her," Lennox said, laughing.

Keane chuckled. "There's an awful lot to like."

"No argument there," Lennox said, "but we have to get off this island in order to move on with anything."

"Right. So do you think the drug smugglers will come back in again?"

Lennox thought for a moment. "Our guy didn't seem to think so, and, if they find the body of his partner floating in the ocean, then the answer is no." He lifted out four fish and said, "That's one for each of us. What do you think?"

"Looks to me like it's time to eat," Keane said, hopping to his feet. "And then we need to pack up and get to the shore and see about leaving this place."

"Yeah, to face the next stage of the mission," Lennox

said. "Sounds like we'll flush out an attempted murderer."

"Stop him from making a second attempt at least," Keane said. "That would not be cool at this point."

"No, because then he'll face you."

"Yeah. In a big way," Keane said, laughing. But inside he knew it was no laughing matter. Ever since Sandrine had mentioned it, something had been in the back of his mind. "When we were talking before, it really cemented the problem she would face heading back again. I hope she's wrong," he said.

"And how will we know?" Lennox asked.

"I'm not sure," he said. "I'm just wondering if maybe his buddy saw something."

"But would he tell? From what you're saying, it seems like they tried to bring the two back together, meaning this guy is a friend of her ex. So would he talk in a deal like this? Especially now, after all this time as buddies?"

"More than likely he'll say he doesn't know what he saw."

Lennox nodded, and they returned to the shelter, where the two women were sound asleep. He started up the little cookstove, while Keane went through the food and laid out what they had left.

"We've got plenty here," he said, "even if we stay another day."

"I hope you don't mean that," Sandrine said.

He chuckled. "So you're awake, are you?" he asked in a teasing voice.

"I am," she said, "but I woke up more chilled than when I went to sleep." Smelling the frying fish, she asked, "Time for breakfast?"

"You'll be sick of fish after this," Lennox said.

She smiled and shrugged. "I'm alive. I'm safe, and you're filling my stomach," she said. "I don't really care, and I'm particularly grateful that you're cooking it first."

At that, he laughed and said, "Well, you're first up."

And, using the same darn lid, she ate while he cooked the next fish. Brenda woke up next. As soon as she was up and settled back in after a trip outside, she sat beside Sandrine. Brenda had a smile on her face and said, "I know it's been a pretty shitty couple days for you guys, but I don't remember very much of it."

"Well, hopefully there won't be much more to remember," Sandrine said.

"Well, I am remembering a lot of it. The whole thing is pretty shocking with everything that happened," she said. "I can't thank you enough for saving my life."

Keane looked over to see her smiling at Sandrine.

"I couldn't do any less," she said.

"Now the question is, would you have done that on your own," Brenda said, "or was it only because Scott pushed you?"

# CHAPTER 10

"DID YOU SEE him?" Sandrine asked Brenda. "I wondered if I had imagined it," she said, "I was standing on the side, hanging on to the lines, and he pushed me in. But I was afraid it was my imagination."

"No," Brenda said. "Remember? I was behind you, so I could see the two of you clearly. I wasn't even sure what I was seeing. But he shoved you in and then stood there, with that look on his face."

"What kind of a look?" Keane asked.

"Anger, joy, fury, almost vengefulness. I don't know. It's hard to say, since I was struggling in the water and, at the same time, trying to comprehend what I'd just seen." She turned to Sandrine. "Can you ever forgive me?"

"For what?" Sandrine asked.

"For listening to Greg and trying to patch you two up again. Obviously Scott is not who we thought he was."

"No," she said. "He certainly is not. Besides, I told you on the boat why I broke up with him. I knew he and Greg were friends, and I didn't want to complicate things for you guys, so I didn't tell you the whole story earlier. I figured just saying that we broke it off and that I was moving on would be enough."

"Greg took that really badly. He thought you guys were perfect together," Brenda said.

"Yeah, except for the part about Scott being a lying cheater and apparently an attempted murderer," Sandrine said quietly.

"What will you do about that?" Lennox asked.

She looked at him in surprise. "What do you mean?"

"What will you do about the attempted murder part?" he asked again, looking serious.

"I don't know," she said. "Is there any point in doing anything?"

"You can't let him get away with it," Brenda said. "He could try it again on someone else."

Sandrine winced at that. "And yet, to go through pressing charges and maybe a trial, when it's just an accusation in the midst of a storm, seems difficult. It could be twisted around so much. I can already hear what the attorneys would do to me. And you, since you're a witness," she said.

The two men were suspiciously quiet.

She looked at them. "What do you guys think?"

Their gazes were steady and strong, but Keane said, "Remember what you said to me earlier? About the things that you value the most?"

She nodded. "And?"

"How would you feel if he killed another woman?"

She glared at him. "Not fair."

"No," he said, "it's not. But maybe you should think about it."

KEANE HADN'T WANTED to bring it up, but, at the same time, they would face it and soon. He was wondering about that as they packed their gear, then got them all to where the coast guard long-range interceptor boat would land to pick them and their gear up.

Lennox called out at the top of his lungs, "Ahoy."

Keane spun to see a boat approaching the small cove. He looked at the two women and said, "Stay here." He raced to the shore. When he recognized one of the coast guard boats farther away, he smiled and waved. It took another ten minutes for them to gain the beach, and, at that point in time, he turned to see the two women and Lennox were halfway to him. When the three uniformed men hopped out, a lot of shoulder slapping and handshaking followed, but they were all good guardsmen and nothing like what Keane had been dealing with so far. "Before we leave, we need a confab," he said.

One of them looked at him and said, "Oh?"

"Yeah. Plus, did you guys bring any body bags with you?"

The officer frowned. "No, I don't think so, although there might be one in the storage kits. Why?"

Keane waited until Lennox joined him, and then, with the women standing and listening, he gave as clear an accounting as he could of what had happened since they'd arrived. All three search-and-rescue men stared at him in shock.

"Seriously?"

Keane nodded. "So the one guy took off, heading around the island to our left," he said. "Presumably he'll go all the way around, then turn south, but I don't know that. His partner's body was dumped in the ocean around the corner, and we have two up here."

The guardsmen just stared at him.

Keane shrugged and said, "Come on. Let me take you

up." He looked at the other officers and said, "You might as well stay here, if you want."

They shook their heads. "No. We're with you all the way."

Sandrine asked Brenda if she wanted to wait alone here at the beach.

"I'll wait with Brenda," Lennox stated.

After getting a nod from Brenda, Sandrine said, "Then I'll come with you too, Keane."

The conversation continued as the men asked question after question. Keane answered as well as he could, and even Sandrine chimed in with any answers she had.

By the time they made it to the small shelter, where Wilson sat with a bullet in his head, everybody stood in a circle of silence around the body. Then Keane pointed to where they had buried Adam. "So we have two here," he said, "and they both need to be taken back."

"Well, crap," the one guy said.

"I know. It hasn't exactly been what we thought we were signing up for."

"And the Zodiac that you took to land?"

"It's around the beach, unusable," he said. "We'll take you there too. But, between here and there, we should find another body around the rocks."

"We can try to retrieve that one." One of the men stepped back and brought out his phone. "I'll walk back to the interceptor and call the cutter. We'll need a second boat out here and some body bags. We'll do a full recovery."

Keane nodded and watched as he walked away.

The other two guardsmen walked into the little shelter, then stepped back out again, studying the makeshift doors. "Somebody went to a lot of effort, yet I can't imagine how long this has been here."

"I don't know," Keane said. "The wood is old but must have been brought here. Those are two-by-fours and one-by-sixes."

The men nodded. "Looks like old barn boards."

"Maybe, but it was built deliberately. Smugglers?" Keane asked.

"It's hard to say. Maybe this was a good place for meetings. I don't know."

"Wow," another said, studying it. "We've seen some interesting islands, but this one takes the cake."

"I'd just as soon get off this one," Sandrine said, yawning. "I admit to feeling a little bit like the ocean waves out there. Kind of battered and blown against the rocks."

Understanding crossed the men's faces. "You've had quite the time of it."

"I have, indeed," she replied.

Keane wondered if he should mention what had happened to her or leave it for her to bring up, when one of the coast guard guys smiled at her and said, "That's okay. You'll feel better when you realize that your boyfriends are on the coast guard ship."

Sandrine stared at him in shock. "Both of them?"

"Yep, both of them."

She glanced toward the shore, where Brenda was. "I'll tell Brenda," she said, shooting Keane a worried look, then racing toward the beach.

"She looked happier for her friend than for herself."

"Yeah. A bit of a story comes with that," Keane said. "It's not really my story to tell, but the guy is her ex-boyfriend," he said. "They broke up a while ago, and the other couple was trying to get them back together on this trip."

The guy whistled. "Well, that didn't go as planned."

"Not even close," Keane said. "And there's more. She believes her ex pushed her off the boat in the first place." Both men stared at him. He nodded. "Again, not my story to tell and I don't know if she's willing to bring it up or to go any further with it, but let's keep an eye on the ex-boyfriend."

"Jesus," the one officer said. "Hasn't she gone through enough already?"

"That's partly why I hesitated to bring it up," he said. "The event was witnessed and independently corroborated by the other girl, by the way."

"Wow, that's crazy. He's been incredibly friendly and seemed worried about her," one man said.

"I hear you," Keane said.

"That doesn't mean a whole lot to me at the moment though," the other man replied.

"Right," Keane said. "But we don't know if it's because he wants to know if she remembers or if he's looking for a second chance to kill her."

"Well, *that* he doesn't get," one said.

"No way," said the other.

"I know. I'm giving you a heads-up, just in case."

"Appreciated," he said. "And you didn't shoot these guys, right?"

He shook his head. "Lennox shot the one buried over there, but that's because Adam was firing on them at the time." Keane pointed to the bullets still slammed into the wooden doors.

"I noticed those," the man said. "What the hell? It's bad enough they ended up in the water in the first place, but to get rescued only to end up on a deserted island like this and have the people who saved your life turn crazy and try to kill you is too much. Not to mention their smuggling buddies coming back and trying to kill you all too."

"It's been a hell of a couple days," Keane said. "They cut my rope when I was rappelling down, so I took a hell of a fall. Lennox got shot and slammed over the head." He studied the man in front of him and the little shelter. "I, for one, won't be sad to leave this place either, and I've been here a lot less time than the women."

"It's amazing, isn't it?"

"It is. Have you been on this island before?"

"Yeah, we've done a couple training expeditions here, but not on this side. We were on the south side."

"Right," Keane said. "It's pretty vast and has lots of different plateaus. Different levels and little pathways. Some man-made but some natural from what I can see."

"Right," the guy said. "We weren't exactly sure of some when we were here before, but, like I said, we weren't in this little cove."

The other coast guardsman added, "I remember riding past it, but I don't recall seeing any shelter up here."

"It's so far up that we wouldn't see it from shore," the first replied.

Just then the other group at the beach walked back toward them. Keane studied Sandrine's face, but she had her head bent toward Brenda, the two of them talking back and forth.

"So, the other one is Brenda, and she's the admiral's daughter?" one of the coast guardsmen asked.

"Yeah, and it's a damn good thing that we found them," Keane said. "Brenda has quite a head injury. She's doing better now, but she's still very weak."

"We can get her to the coast guard ship and give her a medical checkup there," he said. "She can go back with us first."

"Agreed," Keane said.

"Good enough for me," the coast guardsman said. "I guess what we should do is get the women back, and then we'll get the rest of this collected."

Keane nodded, his bags already packed. He said, "You want me to stay here and give you guys a hand?"

"I think, once we get everybody back on the boat," he said, "we'll take a run around to see if we can pinpoint where that body in the water is. There's a chance it's not even close to the island anymore," he said. "The turbulence and currents out here could have taken him anywhere."

"I could see him from up above, and, when I came down, he was already getting churned up, so I'm not sure where he is now," Keane said.

"Right. Let's go." Then he looked at the two women, smiled and said, "Are you good to go?"

"Absolutely," Brenda said. "I wouldn't mind sleeping on an actual bed for a bit."

"Well, we've got a doctor on board the main ship," the coast guard officer said. "He'll take a look at your head and make sure you're good to go. Then we'll definitely find a bunk with your name on it. Not the most comfortable, as beds go, but, compared to the floor of that shelter, you're gonna love it."

"That's the best news yet," she said. "And, as much as I love getting fed, fresh fish would never be my first choice."

"Hey, I thought I did a good job," Lennox said.

She looked at him with half a smile and whispered, "You

did an excellent job. I just happen to hate fish."

At that, he looked at her in shock, then laughed. "Well, you were a good sport about eating it anyway," he said.

"That's because I didn't have any choice," she said. "I knew I needed to eat something in order to keep up my strength. So thank you very much for what you did for us."

"Not a problem," he said. "It was fun."

"If you say so." She smiled and carried on, walking slowly toward the beach.

Keane watched as she went, only to realize that Sandrine stood beside him.

In a low voice, she whispered, "Did you tell them?"

He looked down at her. "I mentioned it. Yes."

She wrinkled her face up at him.

"We'll make sure that you stay safe on the ship," he said. "This guy won't get a second chance to hurt you."

Her shoulders sagged as she looked at the uniformed men. Then asked, "What if I'm wrong?"

"Come on. You heard what Brenda said."

Sandrine sighed and said, "I just wish you hadn't mentioned it."

"I'm sure you do, but remember? *Honesty*, right?"

"Okay, fine. He'll probably avoid me anyway."

"Well, we'll see," he said. "Are you planning on going back with them?"

She shot him a horrified look. "Are you kidding me?"

"Just asking," he said. "Maybe absence made the heart grow fonder."

"Not likely," she said. "Besides, *we* have a thing going."

"We do?" he asked cautiously. But the coast guard guys were ahead of them, making plans, out of earshot, and she had looped her arm through his, as they brought up the rear.

"Obviously," she said, as she raised her face to the sun. "Not exactly sure what this thing is. But it sure eclipses anything I had with Scott."

"Really?" Keane felt inane for not coming up with a better answer. Where was the suave can-do attitude now? But something about this woman always caught him sideways.

She squeezed his hand. "That's okay. Big strong silent types like you don't have to talk much."

"That's not exactly what I was thinking."

"Or am I crazy? Is this my imagination?" She stopped, stepped in front of him and frowned. "Am I?"

"Are you what?" He spoke cautiously, easily recognizing the pitiful yawning silence in front of him.

"Am I off my rocker? Am I crazy to think something is between us?"

He gave her a special smile and whispered, "No. You're not. But I don't even know where you live. I don't know anything about you."

"Yeah," she said. "What if we both don't think that love, honor and loyalty are important?" Her quirky smile meant she was teasing him.

At those words, something inside him settled. He nodded. "You're right. We could both think that lying cheating assholes were people we wanted to spend time with."

She twisted her face up and said, "Ow. Sure glad you're joking. That was a pretty painful experience."

"I'm sure it was," he said gently. "But listen. I'm not the cheating kind."

"Neither am I," she said, then kissed him gently on the cheek. "And see? We've got this thing between us." With that, she entwined her arm with his and walked toward the beach.

# CHAPTER 11

THE TRIP TO the coast guard ship was simple and the transition easy. They were quickly ushered into a medical room, where a doctor waited for them. He gave Sandrine a quick cursory once-over and then sat down for a longer checkup on Brenda. Sandrine stayed with Brenda for support and for further information for the doctor, while they went through what had happened, her injuries and the reactions she had. Sandrine filled in the details of symptoms that occurred while Brenda was unconscious or sleeping.

Finally the doctor nodded. "Both of you had a pretty near miss," he said. "Any which way you look at it, you're lucky to be alive."

"I know," they both said, nearly in unison. And, with that, they were both led to a room with bunks inside. Brenda sagged on the bottom one and said, "I don't know about you, but I'm exhausted."

Still worried about the pale color on her friend's face, Sandrine helped her get under the covers. "Are you sure you don't want to strip off first?"

Brenda shook her head. "No, I'm not that comfortable yet. I just want to sleep." She patted Sandrine's cheek and said, "Thank you for watching over me."

"I'm just so grateful you weren't hurt even worse," she said. "It was pretty rough watching you with blood oozing out of your head and clearly delirious and talking crazy," she said. "But I'm so glad you pulled through." As soon as Brenda seemed comfortable and her eyes started to droop, Sandrine stepped out into the hallway in time to see Keane coming out of a nearby room.

"I wasn't sure if you guys would even stay on board," she said with a bright, welcoming smile.

"Just for a little while. I'm heading out again in a bit," he said. "I just got back from the second boat. We collected a couple bodies."

"A couple?"

His face sobered. "We couldn't find the one in the water."

She groaned. "That'll provide ugly thoughts for my nightmares to feed on."

"I know," he said. "Me too. I'm sorry about that." He looked down the galley. "Are you heading up?"

"I was hoping to," she said. "Honestly I haven't seen Scott and Greg yet."

"That's another issue," he said. "They're here, but I think they're in one of the lounges. They know that you're both on board, but I don't think they've been told anything else."

"The thing is, Brenda's asleep," she said. "She didn't even want to see her boyfriend first."

"Are things okay with them?"

"I'm not sure," she said. "This trip has definitely been a bit of an eye-opener. She buckled under pressure from Greg and agreed to bring Scott on our trip. But, when she heard all of it as to why I broke up with him to begin with, she was pretty angry. Then, after seeing him push me in, I think she's really confused."

"Understood," he said. "Come on. You can come with me," he said. "We'll go on up and see if we can get you a cup of coffee and maybe some real food. Although I'm not sure they carry that much on board."

"A kitchen or something should be here, right?"

"There will be," he reassured her. "At least coffee and maybe some sandwiches."

She smiled. "It's hard to believe it's still morning," she said. "A part of me says I should go crash, but I'm still too keyed up. I feel like I should wait a little bit longer and then have a nap." He motioned for her to walk down the aisle in front of them. She came to the first set of stairs and hesitated. She looked at him, and he smiled.

"Let's go on up."

As she did, she spotted a large lounge off to the side. Computers were available on both sides, and chairs were at one end. A couple men were there working. Not Scott and Greg thankfully. She walked inside the room with Keane at her side, studying the general layout. "This is pretty fascinating." She smiled at the two men.

"It is. We have living quarters on these big coast guard cutters," one man said. "The smaller ones are just for day trips, but these are meant to go out for a few days at a time."

A man in uniform stepped forward to join them. He reached out to shake her hand. "Captain Schmidt, at your service," he said in a gruff voice.

She smiled up at him. "Thank you so much for the rescue, Captain."

He gave a clipped nod in response. "Sounds like you had a difficult experience."

"Definitely. Quite the time of it," she said softly.

A voice came from behind the captain. "Sandrine?"

She looked at Keane. "That'll be Scott."

Suddenly Greg was right here too. He reached out and wrapped her in a gentle hug. "I'm so damn glad you two survived," he said.

Sandrine searched his face but couldn't see any sign of deception. She stepped out of Greg's embrace. "Brenda's sleeping. She's doing better but not feeling very strong yet. It's been an ordeal."

He wiped tears from the corner of his eyes and nodded. "After all she's been through, that's totally okay. Hopefully she'll feel good enough to come up. Otherwise, maybe I can go down." He looked at the captain.

"Maybe later when she's awake but not right now as long as she's sleeping. Rest is what she needs, I'm sure. And I'll speak to the doctor about her condition and check in with her. I'll report more to you later."

Just then Sandrine could see Scott.

He gave her an affable look and a big beaming smile. "I'm so glad you survived that terrible storm," he cried out. He stepped forward and gave her a hug, even though she was stiff and unwelcoming. As soon as he let her go, she stepped closer to Keane to stop Scott from trying another move like that again.

The coast guard captain looked at Sandrine and Scott and said, "Maybe you'd like to tell us all what happened."

"Do I have to?" she asked.

His quick nod convinced her that she might as well get it over with.

She sighed and said, "Yes, of course I do. Is there any chance of a cup of coffee?"

"Absolutely, and I understand Lennox made you some lovely fish for breakfast," the captain said with a grin, completely changing his expression, making him even more approachable.

"Absolutely," she said, "and I was grateful to have it, but, if any other food is here," she said with a smile, "I would appreciate it."

"We can probably find a few things," he said.

She was led over to an area with a comfortable chair and a love seat. She immediately sat in the love seat, and Keane sat beside her.

Scott looked at Keane and asked, "So, are you the guy who rescued her?"

Keane nodded but didn't reach out a hand. "I'm one of a two-man team sent looking for them, yes."

"How did you know where to find them?"

"Wasn't too hard with their last-known GPS location," he said. "We cleared the other islands, then searched that biggest one. We found them in the third quadrant."

"It's amazing they survived it all," Scott said.

"Particularly considering the odds against them," Keane said.

She looked at him. He just gave her a quick smile, but she could see the anger in the back of his gaze. She looked at Scott and Greg and asked, "You guys made it back okay?"

"We made it, but we were hours getting back home again," Greg said. "We made it back to shore and sent out the alarms. We told the coast guard what had happened and that started the circus."

"A circus with a good ending," she said. She sagged into the couch, absolutely loving the fact that she had comfort again. "You don't realize how much you take the simple things in life for granted until you do without them."

Just then a man walked toward her with a tray. A small

table was clicked open in front of her, and the tray placed beside her.

She looked at it and smiled. "Well, I see a lot of food here," she said, laughing.

"You eat whatever you like," the captain said. "We all know what it's like to be without a meal or two."

She nodded. "I really hope I never go through another scenario like that again."

"How bad was it?" Greg asked anxiously.

"Well, it was way worse," she said, "because I had terrible nightmares about the boat and how I ended up in the water," she said smoothly, without even looking at Scott, "plus, being afraid that I would never reach Brenda. ... In the end, I woke up on the island, locked inside this weird little fortress. Some guy turned up, giving me a little plastic container with some fish and some biscuits, telling me how he saved us from drowning and brought us to the island. But then he left, and it just went downhill from there."

"So bizarre," Greg said, shaking his head. "I mean, it's awesome that he saved you and that they put you on the island, but what happened after that? I mean, we only got bits and pieces of what happened."

"Well, I think a lot of it is also Brenda's story," she said. "So maybe we'll wait for a bunch of it until she's up to it, if you don't mind," she said. With that, she picked up the cup of coffee, looked at it and smiled. "Ah, real coffee." She glanced sideways at Keane. "Of course I still really appreciated the cup of tea."

He laughed. "Go ahead and eat," he said. "This is definitely what you've been waiting for."

She hugged the cup, took a sip and just closed her eyes, sagging gently into the corner of the love seat. "Nothing quite like a good cup of coffee." She drank half of it, just holding the cup and sipping. Finally she put it down and looked at the feast in front of her: a breakfast sandwich and several muffins, some pastries, fruit and even yogurt. She picked up the breakfast sandwich and said, "This I will take care of, no problem."

The men had an easy conversation around her as she ate, though she caught the edge in Keane's voice every time he spoke. A definite sense of unrest was in Scott's gaze as he studied her. The captain asked a few more questions, and she answered everything she could. For now. What she hadn't considered was the cost for this rescue. She hated to even bring it up and decided she wouldn't ask about it in the open like that. She would ask Keane about it privately. When she got to the end of the breakfast sandwich, she started in on the muffin, but, halfway through, she knew she couldn't finish it. Putting the muffin on the plate, she handed it to Keane. "Can you finish this for me?"

"Wow," he said, "I figured you'd get more down than that."

She shook her head. "No, and somehow the coffee's making me really tired."

As a matter of fact, with her feet curled up on the couch and a big pillow beside her, resting her body into the corner, she was almost too relaxed. "I probably should go back down and have a nap with Brenda," she said. "I don't really want her to wake up alone either."

"I could go down there," Greg said anxiously.

She looked at him, smiled and said, "Not until the captain says so."

He sagged in his chair and nodded. "I guess that's fair." But he wasn't terribly impressed with the idea.

She looked at Keane and said, "Otherwise, I'll fall asleep right here."

"No, we won't do that," he said. He helped her to her feet, smiled at the rest of the men and said, "If you'll excuse us, she's going below for a nap." Then he slowly led her to the stairs.

"How come I'm so tired now?" she asked. Going down the stairs was almost a chore. He led her back to her room and said, "Part of it is just the end of the adrenaline wearing off. Finally knowing that you're safe and that everything's okay."

"If you say so." She yawned.

He opened the door and checked on Brenda. "She's still asleep." He looked up at the top bunk, then smiled. "Will you get up there okay?"

She nodded. "I'll be fine." She stumbled to the ladder, completely shocked at how absolutely exhausted she was. "Don't let me sleep too late though, please," she said anxiously. "And please don't let Scott come in while I'm sleeping."

He looked at her in surprise. "Do you think he'll try?"

"I don't know, but he'll probably try to come down when Greg does, at least. I don't want either one of them in here while I'm sleeping," she said. "I won't sleep soundly if I'm afraid somebody will come in."

"Well, I can sit here and keep watch, if you want," he said. "I'm pretty sure you'll be fine, but—"

She looked at the small quarters and said, "There isn't any room for you to sit here and wait," she said, "so don't worry about it."

"If I sit in my bunk across the hall and keep the door open, I can see if anybody tries to come in or out of your place."

She looked at him for a long moment. "I hate to ask you—"

He shook his head firmly. "You're not asking," he said. "I just offered."

She smiled, then whispered, "If you wouldn't mind, I'd really appreciate it. I feel like we've been through so much already, and I'm seeing danger where there isn't any. But I don't know. I just felt very uneasy up there."

"Good enough for me," he said. "Now lie down," he ordered in a gentle voice.

She collapsed downward and tucked the pillow up under her head and whispered, "I'm so damn tired."

"So, for that reason, you'll sleep." He stretched up a little bit over the upper bunk to drop a kiss on her forehead. "Now be a good girl and sleep."

She smiled and whispered, "That's one order I'm happy to take." With that, she closed her eyes and dropped off into a deep sleep.

KEANE SAT ON the side of his cabin, without even a chair. In such a very small sleeping area, he was content to just sit in the corner on his phone as he went through the information he had. And that was damn little. He was more concerned about Sandrine's ex-boyfriend and the look on his face when he'd seen her. He had hugged her, and she had allowed it, but stiffly. Of course the fact that she'd snuggled up closer to Keane afterward had warmed his heart.

But he also understood that she was trying to get away from a predator. They'd be home in a few hours, and that was important, so she could get back to a normal life. But what would that mean for her? What would it mean for this boyfriend of hers? *Ex*-boyfriend, he corrected himself mentally. His phone rang just then, and he answered it to hear Lennox on the other end. "The body recoveries are done and stowed, so everybody is heading back to port now."

"Good enough. Do we have an ETA?"

"They're figuring two and a half hours."

"Okay. She's likely to sleep that long anyway."

"And then what?" Lennox asked curiously.

"I don't know," he said. "I guess drop her off at her apartment, a job well done. A weird job but, hey, I'll take it."

Lennox laughed. "So my job to head up next will be a search and rescue too?"

"Hell, they'll probably send you off into the bowels of Africa or some dang thing," he said, laughing.

"Hey, don't say that," he said. "It seems like this one was a bit of an anomaly."

"No, I don't think so. Nico's job was pretty wild too."

"So we're just out there to help whoever needs a hand?"

"Sounds like it," Keane said. "You know I'm okay with that."

"I'm not having a problem with that part of it," Lennox said. "It certainly beats the heavy military drilling. But we have to keep in shape too. We Mavericks don't have the same schedule for that."

"No, I think we'll set that up ourselves."

"Yeah, but one of the best things would be a gym with everybody," Lennox said. "It kept us all motivated and fit as SEALs."

"As Mavericks, we're scattered in a lot of locations," he said, "but, anytime you want to go, just let me know."

"Good to know," he said. "I'll hang up now and talk to a couple of the coast guard guys. They've still got a bunch of questions on the extra visitors we had. … Hang on a minute," he said.

Keane waited, knowing from Lennox's voice that something was up.

"You there? They've spotted another boat up ahead."

"What kind of boat?" Keane asked, standing up.

"A small black Zodiac, but they said it appears to be struggling."

"Any passengers on board?"

"The guardsmen have gone up on deck to see," he said. "I'm standing at the pilot's station. The storm is picking up again."

Keane paced in his tiny space.

"Okay, somebody is on board, but they aren't sure if he's okay or not."

"You know who's coming to mind?"

"Of course. Carlos. The guy who killed his partner and supposedly made a run for a new life."

"Yeah. What are the chances that the smugglers realized he was going in the wrong direction?"

"I wouldn't doubt it," he said.

"I'll be right up," Keane said. Then he stopped. "I promised Sandrine I'd stay here."

"Stay where?" Lennox asked curiously.

"I'm in the room across from where the girls are sleeping," he said. "She said she wouldn't sleep, afraid Scott would sneak in."

Lennox was silent for a moment. "She's that worried?"

"Yeah. But I don't know if it's residual stress from the island or what. No way to tell really until she gets some rest."

"Interesting," he said.

"It is. I'm just not too sure what the end result will be here."

"Okay, well, I've got this. I'll keep you posted."

Just then Keane heard a knock on the door across the hall. Keane hung up the phone to see Greg.

Greg looked at him in surprise and said, "I was hoping to talk to Brenda."

"They're both sleeping," Keane said, motioning at the closed door, to Greg who was still knocking on the women's door. "Did you want something?"

Greg's face fell. "I've been waiting to see her," he said. "It breaks my heart to know that I can't touch her yet."

"I guess that depends on if you had anything to do with her going into the water in the first place."

Greg looked at him in shock. "I would never do that," he said. "I was planning on asking her to marry me."

"Are you still planning on it?" Keane asked.

"Yes. If she'll have me. I know she is quite perturbed with me at the moment. At least she was angry on the sailboat."

"And why is that?"

Greg hesitated, and then his shoulders deflated. "These last few days have been the worst days of my life," he said. "Trying to find out if she was alive or dead, and knowing that she had fallen from my sailboat. It was even worse because the last few hours we had together were so bad."

"How bad?" Keane asked.

"She was mad at me," he said simply, "and I guess I deserved it."

"Mad at you why?" Keane leaned against his door, studying the tall scholarly looking man in front of him.

He did look distraught. "She had gone along with me, trying to get Sandrine and Scott back together again."

"Even though they'd been broken up for two whole months?"

"Scott wanted another chance," Greg said simply. "He's been my buddy for a long time, and I didn't think there was anything wrong with giving them the opportunity to try to work things out."

"If he only needed an opportunity, he could have stopped by her place or called her."

"He tried calling her, but she wouldn't answer. She never seemed to be home whenever he went there, but he figured she wasn't answering the door because she knew it was him."

Keane shook his head, incredulous. "So, even though you knew she'd been avoiding contact with him, you thought it was a better idea to put them both on a boat out in the middle of the ocean where she'd have no choice?"

"I figured at least they'd talk and get it over with," Greg burst out. "I was just trying to help out a buddy."

"And Brenda didn't appreciate that?"

"No. I guess she hadn't known the full story behind why they broke up, so, when Sandrine told her, Brenda got pretty upset with me."

"But you knew?"

Greg shrugged.

"You knew the guy was a cheater and a loser, but you were totally okay trying to hook him back up with your girl's best friend?"

Greg looked at him strangely. "Well, when you say it like that, it's not very nice."

"What other way is there?" Keane asked. "None of this is

nice. She finds her boyfriend in bed with another woman and breaks it off, and, instead of supporting her, you support him, even though he's a cheater."

"He's a guy," Greg said.

At that, Keane just stared at him and then laughed. "Really? Yeah, I'm a guy too, but that doesn't mean I cheat on women."

"Okay. Whatever. He made a mistake," Greg said, trying to backtrack. "He's been a friend for a long time, and we all make mistakes. He wanted another chance, and I was okay with trying to help him get it. That's the end of the story."

"Except that, when Brenda found out, she was angry, upset and pissed off."

"Yeah, she was. She didn't like what I'd done and thought less of me for it. But I got angry too because I didn't like being judged about it. I don't like it now either," he said, clearly angry with Keane.

Keane said. "And did you see how she ended up in the water?"

"Brenda was trying to move closer toward me, and she was hanging on to one of the lines," he said, his face twisting with the memories. "Next thing I knew, a wave came up, and she was gone."

"Life jacket?"

"Oh, yeah," he said. "Everybody on my boat wears a life jacket."

"But you couldn't get back to her?"

"We threw her a life preserver, and I was trying to get the sailboat turned around so I could come back and pick her up," he said.

"And then what happened?"

"And, before I knew it, Sandrine's in the water, heading

toward Brenda. And that was pretty damn stupid."

"Stupid?"

"Well, it's tough enough to rescue one, but now I've got two to rescue."

"Any idea how she ended up in the water?"

"Well, she jumped, I'm sure," he said. "That's Sandrine. She jumps into trouble without thinking."

"You've known her for a long time?"

"A few years, yeah," he said. "Not as long as I've known Brenda though."

"Did it look like she could save Brenda?"

"At that point she might have been doing a better job than I was because I couldn't get back to them. The wind was trashing my sails, and the waves were washing over us, completely hampering our progress. I was tied in, and so was Scott, but we just couldn't seem to get back to them. Next thing I knew, they were gone. We stayed out for a long time while I searched, looking all over for them, but found no sign of either of them. As soon as the storm calmed down, I circled around that area, while we called for help. Then I came back to shore and found the coast guard, and we told them what happened."

"So you must have thought they were dead."

"Of course I did," he said. "What else was I to think?"

Keane shrugged. "They were picked up by two guys," he said, "then carried to shore and left on land."

"Thank God for that," he said. "I don't know how far they must have traveled, because no land was close to us."

"Sandrine hooked their life vests together, and those plus the one preserver was enough to keep them up."

"She would do that," he said, "but apparently Brenda hurt her head?"

"Yes. Which is one of the reasons you're not allowed in their room now," he said.

"She probably hit some rocks. I told you that storm was something else."

"Maybe she hit her head on the boat on the way over?" Keane asked.

"I don't think so," he said. "She was there, and, the next thing I know, she wasn't."

"Brenda or Sandrine?"

"Same thing. Sandrine was standing there, yelling at Brenda, and she's the one who threw the life preserver to get her up. The next thing I know, Sandrine was jumping off in Brenda's direction."

"What kind of a jump was it?"

Greg leaned back slightly and looked at Keane. "What do you mean, *what kind of a jump*?"

"Well, you saw her go in, right?"

"Yeah. I was yelling at her not to do it, yet she looked like she was getting ready. Then I turned to look at Brenda and to see her hand reaching for the life preserver, but she looked pretty weak. The next thing I know, Sandrine's in the water."

"Did she dive in? Did she cannonball? What did she do?"

He frowned and said, "I guess a wave must have hit her sideways or something. Hell, I don't know. Maybe she fell because she didn't go in gracefully. She went a little sideways, with her arms out."

"Almost like she was pushed, huh?"

Greg stared at him for a long moment, and then all his friendliness was withdrawn, and his anger rose up. "You better not be saying what I think you're saying."

"Oh, I'm not saying anything," Keane said, "but I know what these two women said."

Greg looked from Keane to the door hiding the two women and back again. "What the hell are they saying?"

"Where was Scott when Sandrine went in?"

"They were standing together," Greg said, but he shook his head. "No way he would have hurt her."

"No, of course not," Keane said, "because she was completely receptive to his attempts at making up, wasn't she?"

Greg frowned. "No. He was trying hard, and she wasn't having anything to do with it. I got quite angry at her."

"Angry *at her*?" Keane shut his eyes and scratched his head. "So you tricked her into going sailing with an ex she has been very clear about not wanting to be with. She doesn't accept his advances on the boat, for very legit reasons since he's an undisputed cheating, lying sack of shit, and you're mad at *her*? That's messed up."

Greg raised both hands in frustration. "I don't know about that. It just made for a very uncomfortable sailing trip."

"Ya think? And you couldn't see that coming? How is any of that her fault?"

Greg ran his hands over his face. "Look. I don't know what the hell happened. I don't know anything at the moment. I feel like you're putting me on the spot. I didn't do anything, okay? I was trying to help a friend, and maybe that wasn't the best way to do it. And, yes, I was getting angry because I wanted Sandrine to relax and to tell Scott that it was all okay."

"*All okay?*" Keane said, studying this very strange male in front of him. Greg was the opposite of the kind of guys who Keane hung out with. "So, if it's okay for *him* to cheat, does that mean it's okay for *you* to cheat too?"

"No, it's not okay for anybody to cheat," Greg said, "but it happens."

"It happens, and everybody's just supposed to forget about it?"

"Well, she could have been friendly, at least. No reason she couldn't have made an effort to be friendly."

Keane nodded as if it made sense, but, to him, it made no sense at all. "So what did Scott do when Sandrine went into the water?"

"Nothing," Greg said. "What was he supposed to do? No point in a third person going into the water after them."

"Well, why would he go? If she had jumped, surely she would have said something to him."

"Yeah, of course she did. She had a life jacket on, and she did head straight for Brenda," Greg said. "You should talk to Scott about it," he said eagerly.

"Yeah, that's a good idea. Where is he?"

"He's upstairs. You should go up and see him."

Keane crossed his arms, leaned against the doorway and said, "I'm not leaving these women."

Greg started to get angry once more. "It's almost like you think I'll hurt Brenda," he said. "I love her."

"Yeah? But it's okay for your friend to be a cheating, lying sack of shit. You think it's okay to cheat too on the woman you supposedly love, but you're here to make sure that you get a chance to see her."

"Just because he cheated doesn't mean I cheated," Greg said. "And I do happen to love Brenda."

"Ah, okay. So you didn't cheat because you love her, but the other guy cheated so, therefore, he didn't love her?"

Greg looked very confused. "Look. Somehow we got off

into a very strange conversation, and we need to get back on track. As long as Brenda's okay and she's healthy, I'll wait until I can see her."

"Good," Keane said. "Maybe you should send Scott down, so I can have a talk with him."

"Sure," Greg said. He took a few steps away, then turned back. "I just don't understand what capacity you are here in," he said. "You're acting like you're security or something."

"Or something," Keane said softly, very softly. His gaze narrowed as he looked at the tall man, Greg was suddenly looking for a way to retreat.

"And, if I find out that you haven't been faithful to Brenda in these last few years, I'll be having another talk with you too."

"What the fuck, man?" Greg said. "There's no law against having an affair."

"No," Keane said. "But there are morals and ethics, and, you know, honor. Reasons not to do such a thing. But I gather those don't really matter to you."

"It happened way early in our relationship. It's not an issue," he said. "She probably even knows about it."

"Then no reason to hide it, is there?" Keane asked.

"No. No, there isn't. I can talk to her about it later, if it's a big deal," he said, backing down the hallway.

"I guess it depends on if she knows about it or not, right? I mean, you're the one who said she knows."

"I'm sure she does," he said. "Like I said, it was a while ago."

"And what's the lady's name?"

The guy gave him a haunted look and said, "I don't have to tell you that."

"If it was a long time ago, and she already knows about it, what difference does it make?"

"Lily," he murmured as he bolted backward. "Her sister, Lily."

That's when Keane heard a voice behind him.

"What a lying sack of shit," Brenda roared at the open door. "My own sister?"

Keane turned and looked at her with interest and said, "Oh. I guess you didn't know about it, huh?"

# CHAPTER 12

SANDRINE WOKE UP to the sound of Greg's voice. For some reason their door was slightly open letting them hear all that nastiness in clear audio. She lay here, listening to the conversation, almost giggling at Keane twisting Greg's words around and making Greg tell the truth. When she heard that he'd had an affair, it made her sick. But when he admitted it was with Brenda's sister, her heart broke for her friend.

No way in hell Brenda knew about that. She never would have accepted it. Her sister was one who would have never let it be known either. Lily was always the jealous type, always one to be taking toys away from Brenda when they were younger. And it continued when it came to boys. But Sandrine had thought Greg was different and had hoped they had something solid together. Then she heard Brenda below her. First yelling and screaming, then bursting into tears. Sandrine rolled over slowly, and, moving carefully, she hopped down to the bottom bunk, wrapping Brenda in her arms.

Sandrine looked at Keane, who winced at her and quietly mouthed, "I'm sorry."

She shook her head. "We're better off knowing," she said. And that started Brenda bawling her eyes out again.

Sandrine said, "Now that we're awake, you don't have to

stay on your post though."

He nodded and disappeared, closing the door behind him. She hugged Brenda, who was draped in her arms, hot tears rolling down her cheeks.

"How could he do that?" Brenda mumbled.

"It was early, he said," Sandrine muttered. "And you know what your sister can be like."

"And I warned him about that too," she said. "He just laughed and promised me that he didn't like her at all."

"Yeah, but men can be men," Sandrine said sadly. The two women just held each other close.

Finally Brenda sat up. Looking at Sandrine, she took a deep breath. "I don't even know what to do."

"You'll do nothing for a while," Sandrine said simply. "We've both been through a lot. It's been a stressful and traumatic couple of days. We need to go home and let things calm down for a little bit." Stroking Brenda's hair, she continued, "After that, you'll be in a better position to think about how you feel about Greg and what you want going forward. Then you can process all that and find out anything else you need to know."

Brenda nodded and sniffled. "No matter what, he's still a lying sack of shit. And I really do like that phrase."

Sandrine chuckled. "Yeah, it's definitely colorful and obviously hits the spot in some cases." Stretching, she said, "I think we'll be home soon."

"Good," Brenda said. "I'm exhausted."

"Exactly. So let's get you home, then into bed, and maybe, when we're both up for it, we'll do some shopping. Get us a little retail therapy," she said with a laugh. "It's good that you aren't living with him yet. I think you need a few days to yourself."

Brenda sat up, wiped her eyes and whispered, "God, what a shit trip this turned out to be. What a nightmare."

"Yep," Sandrine said. "But at least it's almost over."

In fact, the next couple hours passed quickly, as the two women talked quietly. Before they knew it, Keane was at the door, telling them they were coming into the docks. By the time they disembarked and headed to the parking lot, Keane was already waiting for them up ahead with Lennox. Sandrine looked at Keane and said, "I suppose I say goodbye now, huh?"

He shook his head. "We'll see you both home. Neither of you drove down here, did you?"

"No," Sandrine replied. "I caught a ride with them, and we came in Greg's truck," she said.

"I'm not going anywhere with him," Brenda said. She had steadfastly refused to even talk to Greg. Although he had tried several times, she had just held up a hand and said, "I have some things to think about, and I'm not talking to you until I've done that and until I'm ready."

He had such a crestfallen look on his face that Sandrine almost felt sorry for him. *Almost.* She looked at him and said, "You really shouldn't have had an affair with Lily."

He raised both hands, palms up. "I knew I should have told Brenda," he said, "but I didn't know how."

"You shouldn't have done it in the first place," Sandrine said. "A woman can forgive a lot of things, but something like that—I don't know how they can." With that, she turned and walked away.

Nico was there with a large SUV. He held open the rear passenger door and said, "Ladies, we'll be taking you home."

Sandrine smiled and waited for Brenda to get in, then crawled in behind her. "Have you made contact with

Brenda's father yet?"

"Yes. He's waiting for her at home."

Brenda cried out, "What? He's there?"

Lennox nodded as he got into the driver's side. "Yep. We'll drop you off first," he said. They drove through the traffic, everyone fairly quiet until they got to Brenda's apartment. When they made the turn, they could see her father standing outside her apartment, waiting to meet them. Brenda let out a broken cry as Lennox pulled up. Barely waiting for the vehicle to come to a stop, she opened the door and jumped into her father's arms before anybody could say anything.

Sandrine sat in the back of the vehicle, tears in her eyes. "Will you guys get out and say anything?"

Keane looked back at her and asked, "Are you getting out?"

Sandrine frowned, then shook her head. "No. Look at them." The two had their arms wrapped around each other as Brenda's father led her to the front door.

At that moment, Brenda realized she hadn't said anything and came racing back. "I wanted to say, *Thank you*," she explained.

Sandrine took the moment to hop out and hug her friend. "Get some rest. I'll call you."

Still sniffling, but with a smile on her face, Brenda waved at the two men. "Thank you so much for everything."

Her father lifted a hand, and that was it, and the two walked inside.

Sandrine jumped back in the SUV. "I'm surprised her father didn't thank you."

"He already has," Keane replied. "We spoke to him on the phone earlier."

"Wow." It seemed rather cold to her.

"He's an admiral," Keane said. "We did our job, and he knows it."

"I guess it doesn't matter if you're okay with it," she said. "Just seems like a handshake and a thank-you wouldn't have been out of order."

"But neither is necessary," Lennox said. "So shall we drop you off too?"

"If you must," she said. "I'm not looking forward to going home though."

"What? I thought you were," Keane replied.

She nodded but frowned. "I know. It's just the thought of being alone doesn't thrill me right now."

"Well, I can always drop off Keane too," Lennox said. "I've got to report in and do a couple other things," he said, "but Keane can spend some time, if that's what the two of you decide on."

Keane looked back at her and said, "I wasn't planning on leaving you alone tonight."

She looked at him, relief washing over her. Tears gathered in the corner of her eyes. "Thank you," she whispered. "I know I'll have to get over it soon, and that some would say I don't really have anything to get over," she said. "It's just—it was so goddamn lonely out there."

"Hey, let's get you back home and settled in your own space," he said. "You just need some time, and you'll be fine."

She smiled and nodded. Soon they pulled up in front of her apartment building. She hopped out and patted her pockets, where she had put her house key, so she didn't need a purse when going sailing. "I don't have my key anymore." She stared at the brick building. "It doesn't look like much, does it?"

"It doesn't matter," he said. "It's not about what you live in. It's about who lives there."

She loved that. "I'm glad to hear that. Most of the time people are all about what you own."

"But they haven't lived through something life-threatening. You have," he said. "And you already know that what you own has nothing to do with who you are."

She looped her arm through his and said, "And it's midafternoon, and I'm already exhausted."

"You probably need more food too," he said.

"Well, a solid meal would help," she said. "If I can convince you to stay at my place overnight, maybe we could order in something."

"Or we could go out for dinner," he said.

She looked up at him and whispered, "But that's almost like a date."

He laughed. "Almost," he agreed. "Would you be against that?"

"Hell, no," she said. "I certainly would not. I was hoping to see you again, naturally. After all, we have this thing between us. I just didn't know what the protocol was."

"No protocol," he said. "Just life as we choose to make it."

"It's hard to argue with that," she said.

"Let's get settled in and see how we do. You might just want to go to bed and stay there," he said.

"Maybe so."

At the door, she stared at the lock. "I don't have a key. I used to keep a key under the mat... then decided it wasn't a good idea considering my ass of an ex..."

"Good. And no key is no problem." He reached into his

back pocket and pulled out a small case, then a small tool. Within seconds the door was open. As soon as she got inside, she walked into the living room, looked around and said, "You know what? I really don't like this place."

He laughed. "It took you getting washed out to sea and abandoned on a not-so-deserted island to decide you don't like where you live?"

She turned to look at him. "I know it probably sounds foolish, but I think it's more a case of suddenly wanting to change things that may have bothered me before, but I wasn't willing to make the effort." She glanced around the apartment, shrugged and said, "I need a shower and a change of clothes."

"Do you have any coffee?"

"Oh, of course," she said. "Coffee." She headed into the kitchen, put on a pot, then turned to face him. "Did you bring a bag or anything?"

He pointed at the bag by the door. "I've got my laptop and stuff in there," he said. "I have some work to do."

She beamed. "So, are you okay if I have a shower?" she asked hesitantly.

His eyebrows shot up. "Why wouldn't I be?"

She shrugged irritably. "Never mind."

"Wait. Does it have something to do with Scott? No, don't answer. Just let me tell you something about me. This is your home. You can take a shower or do anything else any damn time you please. And the day I have a problem with it is the day you should throw my ass out." Taking her gently by the shoulders, he turned her and pointed her in the direction of the hallway. "Go get a shower. You'll feel better."

"That I will. Thank you." She headed down the hall and

into the bathroom. Turning on the water, she quickly got undressed.

When she stepped into the hot water, the whole sensation was such a shock to her system that she stood there shuddering, her body enjoying the hot water streaming over her. The last few days—exposed to the sun, sand, salt water and wind—had dried out her skin, and she still felt like she had sand everywhere. She was reminded of her early attempts to even relieve herself in that difficult environment. Not exactly her finest hour. Hopefully she wouldn't have any other chance to practice.

She quickly scrubbed herself down, washed her hair twice, scrubbed herself once more, and, when she finally felt clean again, she turned off the water and wrapped herself up in a big towel, grabbing another for her hair.

As she stood here in front of the mirror, she realized fatigue was once again draining her. But was it relief or fatigue or just the shock and adrenaline release now that she was home? Something had shifted, at least.

She made her way back into the bedroom and sagged onto the side of her bed. It was supposed to be just a nice day out on the boat with her friends. Just the three of them. But instead, it ended up being four of them, and even now she didn't know for sure what she wanted to do. The fact that Brenda had independently backed up what Sandrine had said was huge. But what did Greg say?

She dressed in some shorts and a T-shirt, then walked barefoot into the living room. Keane looked at her with a smile and said, "You look like you're eighteen."

"Well, you can add a decade to that," she said cheekily. "Thankfully I'm a few days older than I was when I went off that boat."

He nodded in understanding. "Nothing like a brush with death to make you rethink your life."

"Have you ever come close to dying?"

"Several times," he said. "I was a Navy SEAL for a long time, so I was in and out of dangerous situations often. I've never come close to drowning though. I did go parachuting and ended up with my chute not opening once," he said. "Thankfully it was a training session, and I survived. I've been shot several times and stabbed too."

She gasped, and her eyes were wide and round. "What?"

He shrugged. "Like I said, it makes you a little more aware of what's going on in your world, and a little happier to do the things you need to do. I find it makes me a little less tolerant of bullshit as well."

"Right," she said. "So what I'm feeling isn't all that odd?"

"Not at all," he said. "Expect it, and realize that it's a normal response to an abnormal situation. You will recover from this and will come away with a different perspective, which isn't a bad thing."

"I guess not," she affirmed. "I suppose I won't realize in what ways until a few days have gone by."

"Probably longer," he said. "You'll start to think about the things that are important in life. Things that you still want to do."

"I was thinking about that when I was on the beach, waiting to see if Brenda would survive or die," she said. "I thought of all the things I still wanted to do and what I would regret the most if I didn't get rescued. And I thought what I would change if I got a second chance."

"See? That's all really normal," he said. "Now that you have your second chance, what will you do with it?"

"That'll take some thinking."

"Well, you've already done something," he said. "You've broken things off with your boyfriend."

"But I did that before," she said with a smile. "That was a pretty easy decision."

"Nothing he said while you were sailing convinced you to consider going back with him? Greg said Scott got angry because you were being difficult."

"I was, in a way," she admitted. "I was really angry that they had finagled that whole scenario in the first place. Scott was pressuring me to come back and wanted me to say I forgave him and all the rest of it right there on the spot, and of course I couldn't do that," she said. "Finally I'd had enough. I started yelling and told him that I didn't want anything to do with him, that I'd have never gone on that trip if I'd known he'd be there and that he was the last person I wanted to spend time with."

"Fair enough," Keane said. "How did Greg react?"

"He snapped at me and said I shouldn't be so childish. He said that men had affairs. That's what they did, and I should forgive Scott and get on with it."

"Wow," Keane said. He tilted his head to the side and said, "Well, that pretty well lines up with what he told me in the hallway."

"Right? What I don't know is what Brenda will do now."

"Again, she needs time," he said. "It had to be really hard for her to hear that information, especially after all the trauma she'd been through already. And the trauma will put things in perspective."

"Right," she said. "I hope she ditches Greg."

He chuckled. "Why? Because he had an affair?"

"Because he had an affair and because he had it with her sister of all people and because he's lied about it all this time. And, if he did it once, he'll do it again," she said with a shrug. She walked to the coffeepot, grabbed cups from the cupboard and poured two cups, handing him one.

"Let's go sit outside on the small deck."

She led the way to a small deck off the living room. She sat in one of the two chairs and, with a huge sigh of relief, tilted her head back and lifted her feet so they rested on the railing. "That's it. I'm here for the night." She chuckled.

"Will you ever go sailing again?"

She had to stop and think about it. "I don't know. It was pretty traumatic."

"Have you done much sailing?"

"Yes, and no. I had gone out with them many times, but I've never been sailing on my own."

"So you might like it under the right circumstances?"

"Maybe in a bigger boat. A much bigger boat," she said. And he immediately started to laugh. She looked at him and grinned. "You're really easy to be with, you know?"

"GOOD," HE SAID. He reached out a hand immediately, and she reached back. They sat like that, quiet and comfortable for the longest time. He wondered what he was getting into. "So, are you over the breakup with Scott?"

"I was over the breakup the minute I realized what had happened, and even more so as I managed to get through the actual act of breaking up," she said. "That was more traumatizing than anything. It took a while to recover from the betrayal afterward, from a man who was closer to me than anyone else. But, once I realized he was a cheat, I was done with him emotionally."

"But do you regard all men like him?"

She rolled her head and looked at him and said, "Meaning, do I see you the same as Scott is? No."

"So, if we went out for dinner tonight, you might be okay with that? If you're feeling up to it, that is."

"I'd be totally okay with that," she said with a bright smile. She sat back, did a self-assessment and said, "Yeah. I think I'm strong enough to go out. And maybe that's a perfect plan. Go out for a nice dinner and then come back and finally get a good night's sleep."

"That's probably a good idea."

"The police, they won't need me for anything, will they?"

"Yes, they probably will," he said. "I'm not exactly sure to what extent, but it's quite possible."

"*Ugh*," she said. "I was hoping it would end with the coast guard."

"Maybe, at least if we're lucky. But otherwise it won't be that big of a deal."

"Well, there's no point in worrying about it now," she said. "I'll deal with it if I have to."

"That's the way to do it," he said, just as his stomach gurgled.

She looked at him and gasped. "Of course you're hungry," she said. "You haven't eaten, have you?"

"I have but not a whole lot."

"Where do you want to go for dinner?" He named a popular steak and seafood place close by. She nodded and said, "I'll get changed." She hopped up and walked back inside again.

"Don't change for my sake," he said.

She stopped, looked at him, frowned and said, "Really?"

He raised his eyebrows. "I can't change. I'm wearing the only clothes I brought with me," he said.

She smiled, walked back over and said, "Do you think the restaurant will let us in?"

"They'll let us in just fine."

She laughed and said, "Okay, prove it to me."

He grinned, then hopped up, grabbed his wallet and his phone, and sent a text message to Lennox to tell him what they were doing. Then he headed out the front door with her laughingly towed behind him. "Do you have a car?"

"I do," she said with a grin. "It's not fancy, but it does the job."

"That's fine," he said. "But we're close enough to walk. I thought maybe it would be good to get out for a bit."

"Walking is a great idea."

As they walked, she suddenly said, "I told the captain. About being pushed."

"I heard," he said comfortably.

"I'm afraid now that I shouldn't have."

"Why is that?"

"Because I'm sure it's gotten back to Scott."

"Won't matter as I told Greg the same thing. He was supposed to send Scott down to talk to me while we were still on the cutter, but that didn't happen."

"I don't really want to face him over it."

"Maybe not," he said, "but do you know if there is any chance that he overheard the fact that Brenda saw him?"

"I don't know," she said. "Maybe Brenda said something to Greg, but I'm not sure when that would have been."

"Or to her father."

"Right," she said. "I really didn't want to open that can of worms."

"The can of worms is open," he said. "The question is, what will you do about it?"

"I don't know," she said. "I guess I was hoping to avoid the whole thing."

He smiled and nodded. He worried about it though because he didn't know what Scott's basic character was. "Is Scott likely to be vindictive?"

"He certainly won't appreciate anybody accusing him of trying to knock me off the boat," she said. "I'm sure he'll try to spin it as a joke."

"Some joke."

"I know," she said.

"Well, how about we forget all about it for now," he said, as he led her across the street and into the restaurant. Inside, they were given a table and spent the next two hours thoroughly enjoying their meal and each other. He really liked who she was as a person. He didn't know that he'd ever pick her out of a lineup as being somebody that he'd enjoy spending time with, as he tended toward brunettes. She was a blonde. As he got to know her, her real beauty started to shine.

By the time they were ready to head back home again, he tucked her arm into his elbow and led her outside.

She yawned. "I'm sorry."

"Come on. Let's get you to bed."

She yawned once more and said, "I'm so damn tired."

"I know. That's understandable. You'll be fine. You just need a little time." They walked slowly all the way back, and she let him into the apartment.

Once inside, she turned and said, "I'm just too tired all

the time now."

He placed a finger against her lips and whispered, "I know. Go on."

She smiled, hooked her arms around his neck and gave him a big hug.

He held her close, surprised but delighted, loving the feel of her warm and sexy body in his arms, but knowing that nothing would happen right now. She was too exhausted and confused for anything right now.

She kissed him gently. "Thank you for a wonderful evening," she said, then slowly made her way to the bedroom and closed the door.

He pulled out his laptop and settled at the kitchen table. First he sent Lennox a text message, saying they were back and that she was safely locked inside again. When his phone rang, he pulled it out. "Lennox, what's up?"

"You clear?"

"Yeah, she went to bed."

"I got a phone call from the admiral," Lennox said. "He called me about ten minutes ago."

"What's up?"

"He was taking Brenda back to his place," he said, "over in the Hillcrest area. Anyway, they had just barely gotten out of the parking lot, and they were involved in a head-on collision."

"Oh, Jesus," he said, straightening. "Is Brenda okay?"

"Well, maybe *head-on* is not quite the right word," he said. "Basically a vehicle smashed into the passenger side, right where Brenda sat. She's been taken to the hospital, banged up but okay. The hospital's keeping her overnight because of her other injuries and all. The admiral has posted two security guards as well."

"Security guards?" Keane's voice hardened. "Are we thinking this was deliberate?"

"The admiral said the other vehicle, which was driving on his side of the road, suddenly came across the center line and targeted the passenger side."

"So somebody tried to kill her?"

"That's what he's afraid of. He's opening a full investigation and has already found out that the vehicle was stolen."

"From where?"

"The same apartment building where Brenda lives."

Keane sat back and thought about that. "God, she just gets back after a trauma like nearly drowning, then the bullshit afterward with Greg, and now gets attacked?"

"Yeah. So then came the question of why."

"Of course, the first off the top of my head is the smugglers," he said.

"Exactly. That guy we let loose in his Zodiac, by the way? The other rescue boat did locate it and our smuggler. Dead, with a bullet between the eyes."

"Wow," Keane said. "Talk about tying up loose ends."

"What are the chances somebody else was on that island?" Lennox asked.

"It's definitely possible," Keane said. "We knew that. Honestly, half a dozen people could have been there if they were familiar with the island and knew what they were doing. We could have been under watch the entire time."

"There's a disconcerting thought," Lennox said.

"I know, right? Now the question is, where and how do we find out who was after Brenda tonight? I doubt the smugglers followed us all the way back to her apartment." But then he stopped. "Shit. I mean, we could have been followed all the way back," he said.

"I didn't see anyone," Lennox said. "But, if they wanted to make sure she didn't survive that trip to the island, that's one hell of a way to do it."

"Nobody else survived," Keane said.

"The four of us did," Lennox said, "but that's it."

"Great. Obviously, if Brenda's in the hospital under guard, Sandrine is potentially in danger as well."

"Which is why I'm calling," Lennox said. "Brenda's dad couldn't identify the driver, but it was a lone male."

"Well, that's something, but that could be the smugglers, or it could even be her stupid ex-boyfriend, Greg."

"*Ex*-boyfriend?"

"Well, I don't know that Brenda broke up with him *yet*," Keane said. "If she was smart, she would. Sandrine thinks she should. But the two of them haven't had any time to talk. I've been with Sandrine the whole time, and Brenda's been with the admiral."

"But still, it's quite likely that's what she would have done. Especially if Greg kept trying to contact her when she made it clear she wanted some alone time."

"But that's not a reason to kill her."

"No," Lennox said. "I'm down at the hospital now, and I'm hoping to ask both her and her father some questions."

"Well, maybe you should come here afterward," Keane said. "I'll stand watch on Sandrine tonight. She's gone to bed now that we're back from dinner, but I wouldn't feel good about leaving her alone until we find out what's going on."

"Yeah, you definitely need to stay there. I'll be by in a couple hours to give you a break on watch."

"Well, check in with me when you're done at the hospital," he said. "I'll see what's happening here."

"Hopefully nothing," Lennox said.

"I hope so," he said, "but I'm not that confident at the moment."

"Later, man," Lennox said as the hung up.

Keane put away his phone, his mind spinning. He looked up to see Sandrine standing nearby.

"What was that?" she asked. She wore the tiniest of nighties with little spaghetti straps.

Not only did it not hide a damn thing, it seemed to highlight every damn thing that he wanted to see. He swallowed hard and closed his eyes for a moment. "Do you mind putting on a robe?" But she either didn't hear him or didn't understand.

"What was that? What's going on with Brenda?"

He groaned. "That was Lennox. He's calling from the hospital. At Brenda's bedside in fact."

"What's wrong with her?" Sandrine cried out, rushing forward. "Is she okay?"

"She's okay," he said, "but there's been an incident."

Sandrine stared at him in shock—her jaw literally dropping. "What kind of an incident?"

He motioned toward the table, and she sat across from him, her hands immediately reaching for his. Trying to avoid seeing her plump breasts right at the edge of the table, he swallowed and kept his gaze on her face. "She and her father were in a hit-and-run accident."

"What?"

He explained what Lennox had said, and she sank back in shock.

"She survives nearly drowning in the ocean, being injured and stranded on a deserted island, drug smugglers trying to kill her, and, after she finally makes it home, somebody tries to run her down a block from her apartment?"

"Not exactly. Sounds like both vehicles were driving on a small side street, but the admiral felt the driver seemed to accelerate and to target her position in the car when he rammed it."

"My God!" she said, huge tears welling up in her eyes. "What is going on?"

"Well, one of the first thoughts that Lennox and I were just discussing," he said, "is whether the drug smugglers knew anything about her, and we wondered if they had decided to cross off more loose ends."

She stared at him uncomprehendingly.

"After we got picked up off the island, as we were underway, we saw a boat floating out in the ocean," he said. "The second coast guard boat went to check it out and identified the one smuggler that we had seen earlier on the island."

"The one that left after shooting his partner?"

"Exactly."

"And was he alive?"

"No, he wasn't. He'd been shot between the eyes."

"But why though? So he couldn't say anything?"

"Yes, and probably as punishment for leaving the smuggling profession. Jobs like that are permanent. They probably assumed that he was trying to take off. Or maybe they had a conversation with him first. I don't know. But the end result is that he's dead."

"So they definitely were eliminating outstanding threats to their operation."

"Exactly. So the question is, did they know that you and Brenda were there, and are they trying to take down the rest of their loose ends?"

"Jesus," she said, staring at him in shock. "Does this ever end?"

He nodded. "It does. Just not as fast as we had hoped."

"Do you really think that's likely?" she asked, speaking slowly. "The only ones who saw our faces are dead now."

"The only ones who saw your faces *that you know of*," he said quietly. "Lennox and I were just discussing whether somebody else could have been on that island. Who maybe didn't know we were there or where we were at."

"But, if we didn't know they were there, and they didn't know about us," she said, "why would they care if we lived or died?"

"Because it could be a place they use on a regular basis," he said, "and maybe they want to make sure nobody'll keep sniffing around their operation."

# CHAPTER 13

"THAT IS JUST so bizarre," she whispered.

"I know," he said. "But it is what it is."

She shook her head. "I need to go to the hospital and see her."

"No," he said. "You need to stay here, safe and sound."

She jutted her jaw out at him.

He grinned. "Lennox has gone to the hospital to see what's going on. The admiral has hired two security guards to make sure Brenda stays safe there."

"None of this makes any sense," she said, feeling bewildered. "We just went sailing for one stupid day."

"And sometimes you cross paths with all the wrong people," he said.

"Exactly," she said. "And now what?"

"Now we wait," he said. "You go to bed and sleep until morning, when hopefully we'll have more answers. Lennox or I will be here all night. We also must consider the possibility that it could have just been an accident."

"Because we're all hypersensitive and think the boogeyman's turning up in every corner?" She liked that idea. But somehow she knew it wouldn't be that easy.

"Listen. I have to ask you this. Would Greg do anything like this?"

She stared at him in shock. "I don't know," she said.

"I'm clearly not the best judge. I wouldn't have thought he would sleep with Brenda's sister or go with the 'all men are cheaters' defense. Hell, I wouldn't have thought he'd set me up to ride on the 'happily ever after' sailing adventure."

"Got it. I understand," he admitted. "And why would he try to hurt Brenda now?"

"Only in rage," she said. "It doesn't make any sense any other way."

"Right," he said. "Okay. So I really suggest you go back to bed and see if you can get some rest. Lennox will call me after he's learned whatever he can at the hospital."

"Nobody could identify the driver? If it was Greg, Brenda should have seen him, right?"

"Apparently she was lying back a bit, with her eyes closed, when they were hit. By the time the admiral managed to get his wits about him, the driver was already long gone."

"And the vehicle?"

"Stolen from the same apartment complex she lives in."

As he watched, Sandrine shoulders sagged. "I don't want to believe it was Greg," she said, "but I just don't know anymore."

Keane stood. Tugging her to her feet, he wrapped her in his arms and said, "Go on back to bed."

"I can't sleep now," she said, staring up at him. "You can't possibly think that'll work?"

"I know, and I'm sorry," Keane said. "I was hoping you would sleep and find this out in the morning, after we knew more."

"I don't want to find this out any time of day," she said, but she did turn and head toward the bedroom. "God." Not getting far, she collapsed on the couch in the living room and said, "It makes no sense at all."

"I know," he said, "but look. You still need to try to sleep," he said.

She shook her head, yet she wandered back to the bedroom. "I just hate to think of Brenda and all she'd been through. I can't believe it's Greg," she said.

"So who else?" he asked, leaning against her doorway.

She loved the look of him here. She looked back at her bed, then at him and said, "I know one way to put this all out of my mind."

He shook his head. "Oh, no. I won't be an exercise to help you forget the things going on in your life," he scolded lightly.

She smiled. "Maybe not," she said, "but you know it's something that you and I both want. And right now, I sure as hell would appreciate something to take my mind off all this." With a shrug, she crawled into bed. "It's a pretty shitty world out there."

"You don't have to be part of it to that extent," he said.

"Bullshit," she said, surprising them both. "It's already on my plate, so what am I supposed to do about it now?"

He frowned.

She nodded. "Exactly." As she lay here, she looked up at him and said, "What if it was Scott?"

His mouth formed a tight grim line as he shook his head. "We can't try to cram somebody into the role," he said slowly, "just because we would like it to be him."

Well, he was right that she would like it to be Scott. She was so done with that man. "What if he heard that Brenda had seen him push me?" At his indrawn breath, she nodded. "I don't know how he would have heard that, or maybe he didn't know for sure," she said. "I'm grasping at straws. But, if he found out what she saw, maybe, by taking her out of the equation, it becomes my word against his."

"And if he tries to take you out again?" Keane asked.

She stared at him and swallowed hard. "Jesus, I don't like this theory." She sat up against the headboard, grabbed her covers and pulled them up to her chest. "So, if it is him, how do we find out?"

Keane had his phone out and was walking into the other room, probably talking to Lennox.

She groaned and dropped her head against the headboard. She really did want him in bed with her, but not just as a teddy bear for comfort for the night.

As she lay here, staring at the balcony, she remembered something else. She got up slowly and went to the glass doors. Opening them, she stepped out. She stood there for a long moment, and, reassured that nobody was here, she finally stepped back into her bedroom.

Keane stood there, staring at her. "What's the matter?"

She shrugged and then said, "I just remembered that one time we were locked out of the apartment. Scott managed to get in by climbing onto the balcony."

His eyebrows shot up, and he strode over to the balcony and looked down. "You're on the second floor, and those trees are too damn close."

"And," she said, "look. Dumpsters over there by the lower patio, and they have that long trellis there."

He looked at it and nodded. "Still a bit dodgy but, if it doesn't work, that's a short fall to recover from."

"But that would mean we were thinking that he might try to break in."

"Well, who knows at this point?" Keane said. "And why would he need to, if you'll leave him a key under a mat?" he said, raising his eyebrow and shaking his head. "Greg told me that Scott tried to call you multiple times and tried to come see you, and you didn't answer."

She frowned at him. "I didn't answer the phone calls, but I don't know anything about him ever coming here. I didn't know he even knew where I was living since we broke up two months ago."

"Have you noticed any trouble?"

She shook her head. "No, nothing. And, for the record, I just stuck that duplicate key there because I wasn't taking my purse or anything on the sailing trip."

"I don't know," he said. "Is everything still the way it's been? Any valuables missing?"

"Everything's the same. No, nothing's missing that I've noticed." She studied where his focus landed, places oddly inconsistent with his questions. She looked up at him. "Come on. Something is on your mind. What is it?"

"The reasons why a boyfriend who doesn't want to break up with somebody might come into her place."

"And you're thinking what?"

"Video cameras," he said bluntly.

The color drained from her face, and she felt her stomach sinking. She sagged down on the bad. "What for?" she asked faintly.

"To put on the internet for revenge is one thing," he said. "For his own personal voyeurism is another."

She buried her face in her hands as she thought about it. "I haven't noticed anything, but can you check?"

"I'll check now," he said. "But tomorrow morning, let's get these locks changed." As he looked at the balcony, he frowned and said, "On second thought, how about you just move? This place isn't very secure."

"Right," she said. "I really don't like this apartment anyway."

"You don't really need anything else to give yourself permission to move," he said; then he went through the apartment. When he came back, he shook his head. "I don't see anything."

"Oh, good, thank you," she said. "You hear such nightmares about an ex posting sex pictures to humiliate their partners and things like that."

"Did he ever take videos or pictures of you like that?"

She shook her head. "No, it's not my thing," she said slowly. "I've always been a little worried about that."

"Good thing," he said, "and we don't know for sure that he had ever done that before, in your former apartment or his, when you were together. Guys with bruised egos aren't always that truthful with their friends."

"Right," she said, giving her face a scrub. "You'll stay for the night, right?"

"Yes, and, should I need to leave, Lennox will come over," he said.

"And you'll call me if Brenda's condition worsens? Or if she needs me?"

"I promise," he said.

"Okay then, I'll try to sleep because it sounds like I'll have a lot to do tomorrow. First thing I'll do is give notice and find a new apartment."

"Let's get you through tonight first," he said.

"But seriously, I don't want to be here any longer than I have to." And, with that, she dropped her head onto her pillow and waved her hand.

"Does that mean *goodbye, get out of here* or what?" he asked with a smile.

"Well, I'd ask for a good-night kiss, but that would be

too dangerous."

"I wouldn't mind a good-night kiss," he said, his voice thickening. When he came over and dropped down beside her, he gave her a gentle kiss.

She wrapped her arms around his neck. "A real kiss would be better."

By the time he kissed her for real, and he finally lifted his head, they were both panting. "Jesus," he said, dropping his forehead to rest on hers.

"I know," she said, sliding her tongue along his mouth and just inside the edge of his lips. "So much damn heat is between us."

"It's not always like this," he said, gently kissing her on her cheeks and her chin. "And this doesn't change anything. I won't be just a fling to get you through the night."

"You're not a teddy bear to comfort me tonight," she said. "You're somebody I want to spend some time with. To figure out if what we have can go anywhere. And that's not a surprise to you."

"No," he said. "That definitely isn't, and neither is this." And, with that, he kissed her harder.

She wrapped her arms tighter and clung to him. Her body twisted as she realized one of Keane's hand had reached under the covers to come up and cup her breast. "You're playing with fire," she said. "I'm already so damn hot that, if you aren't coming to bed with me, you need to back up several paces."

He chuckled. "I don't think I can, Sandrine," he whispered.

When he slowly withdrew his hand, she grabbed it, then gently placed it back. "Please stay."

He took several long, slow breaths, and she knew he was

reaching for control.

She slid a hand down his chest, his abs, to the ridge just under the heavy denim fabric of his jeans and gently stroked him. "Why not?" she whispered.

"Because it's not the right thing to do."

"You think I'm traumatized and I'm not going into this with the right emotional balance or something?"

"Something like that," he said, arching when her fingers wrapped around his ridge. "But you're really shaking my resolve."

"It needs to be shaken," she said. "It needs to be shaken a lot."

He stared down at her, feeling torn. She didn't know how to convince him to stay.

"You know this is what we both want," she said. "And I don't want it just for tonight."

"We'll see," he said, leaning down and kissing the side of her neck, before nibbling his way up to her earlobe as he gently sucked on the end. She twisted her hand, sliding down to reach around his buttocks and squeezed. He swore as she laughed and pulled his T-shirt up above his belly and over his head. And, just like that, he stood, chucked his jeans, and he said, "If you're sorry in the morning—"

She threw the covers back and kneeled on the bed and said, "I'm just sorry we wasted the last three hours," she said. "You know we could have ordered takeout and had it delivered."

He laughed, but he stood in front of her, completely nude, proud, erect and so damn male that she almost panted with need.

She shook her head. "I don't think I've ever wanted somebody as much as I want you right now," she whispered.

"You're so damn gorgeous."

"Hell, no, I'm not," he said. "You're the one who is."

As he stepped forward, she wrapped one hand around his erection, and the other was already sliding up over his chest. "You are gorgeous," she whispered. "You can't lie about something like that." His muscles clenched under her touch. She leaned over and gently kissed the tip of his erection, hearing him groan as she let her tongue play at the top and then slide down ever-so-gently.

Suddenly she was picked up and tossed on the bed. "Playing with fire will get you burned," he whispered.

She groaned as he slowly lifted the nightie up past her hips, his gaze burning deep when her hips and belly were exposed up to her breasts.

Then he lowered his head and took one of her nipples into his mouth, sucking deep and sending a heavy pulse through her lower abdomen. And then his hand slid down to cup her most intimate parts, playing with the moisture already gathered there.

She pulled the nightie over her head and tugged him down to her. "I want more," she said. "I want it all."

"Greedy much?"

"Very." She used her hands, her tongue, as she stroked and kissed her way down, gently cupping his balls below his erection, stroking, tasting his body with her tongue, and wrapping herself over and around as she tried to explore every bit of him.

Finally he captured her traveling hands and tugged her up so she straddled him. "Easy," he said.

"I can't," she said. "There is no easy right now." She reached down and positioned his erection as she slowly lowered herself onto his shaft. He groaned but held himself still as she settled deeper and lower, adjusting to the size of him. She arched backward. "How do you feel about riding?"

"Go, baby," he said, "ride away."

She slowly lowered and raised herself a couple times, then leaned forward and placed her hands on his shoulders and started to ride. And, with a natural movement she didn't know she had, she rode them both to the cliff. And just when she thought she wouldn't make it, he grabbed her hips and ground himself higher up before exploding inside her. Tremors echoed all the way through her, setting off even more tremors as her own climax ripped from one end to the other.

She cried out in shock, and he held her firm, whispering to her to let it go. She tumbled into a massive chasm of exploding color in his arms. Gently weeping, she lay against his chest, amazed, delighted and overwhelmed. "That," she whispered, "was fantastic."

His chuckle rumbled through his chest, making her smile as she stroked the inside of his thighs and then the outside of his hips.

"You are a marvelous male machine," she whispered.

"Ditto," he whispered. "Very female, obviously."

She chuckled and shifted upward slightly, and he left her body. He pulled the blankets over them, settled her beside him, and whispered, "Now will you sleep?"

"If you'll be here when I wake up so we can go for round two, then, yes."

"I promise."

"I'm still stressed," she murmured, "but I feel so much better."

"Sleep," he grumbled, wrapping an arm around her.

She closed her eyes and immediately slept. She woke several hours later, Keane's two fingers busy between her legs, and gradually came to consciousness.

"I couldn't wait," he whispered. As he slid inside her from the back, he took her on a long and slow rise to temperatures almost as hot and as fast as the first time, but the dropping-off-the-cliff was smoother, easier and so damn emotional. She had tears in her eyes when he was finally done, and her body lay trembling in his arms.

"Sleep," he ordered.

She closed her eyes for a second time and fell asleep.

KEANE OPENED HIS eyes, hearing something off. It took a moment to reorient and to determine where he was. But still hearing that inner voice, he grabbed his phone and sent Lennox a text, asking if everything was okay. The answer came back immediately.

**Yeah. At the hospital, still standing guard. Didn't want to leave yet**, Lennox explained.

**So you're not headed here?** Keane confirmed.

**Not immediately. Why?** Lennox replied.

**It means, it's not you who I hear.**

Slipping out of bed, Keane pulled on his boxers and jeans, checking outside the balcony's glass doors to find nothing. The bedroom door was open just a fraction. He had no weapon with him, as he hadn't had a chance to take the gear out of the vehicle Nico had dropped them off in.

Keane nudged the door open ever-so-slightly and slid down the hallway, where he could look at the living room. It was empty too. But then he heard the sound again. And, even as he watched from the corner, he could see the front door slowly open. He watched and waited as the man crept in and closed the door behind him.

He had ropes with him, which was not a good sign. He laid everything down on the kitchen counter and took off his jacket as if preparing to relax or at least to get to work. Then he slipped through the kitchen to the living room.

Not sure exactly what this guy thought he was doing, Keane then saw the handgun. He sucked his breath back because now a confrontation was out of the question. He backed up ever-so-slowly toward the bedroom. From the shadows he couldn't see the man's face either. As the intruder came around the corner, it was all Keane could do to duck back out of sight in the bedroom, but he was also on the far side, where he couldn't make it behind the bedroom door now. He crept to the closet as the man stepped into the bedroom. He had the ropes in his right hand. The mask he wore hid his face.

He was white and about five-ten and lean, maybe 180 pounds. That was all Keane could see. But he heard the voice.

"Wake up, you stupid bitch! Wake up!" He reached down and smacked Sandrine on her feet.

She woke up in shock, then looked at him and screamed.

He grabbed her ankle and gave it a hard slap. "Stop screaming," he said. "I've already got enough lessons I have to teach you. I don't want to sit here and shut your mouth up too. But, if you don't stop, I will."

She immediately stopped, grabbing deep, gulping breaths. "What do you want?" she cried out.

"What do you think I want, bitch?" he said. "I want you to fucking die."

She stared at him in shock.

Keane waited for his chance, but, from where he was, he didn't have a clear move. He didn't want her to get hurt, and he didn't want that damn gun to go off. But the guy was now pacing back and forth at the end of her bed. If he would just walk a little closer to the closet, Keane would have him.

"Why do you want me to die?" she asked. "I've never done anything to you."

"You were supposed to die in that goddamn boat," he snapped.

"What?" Slowly she pulled her legs up and kneeled with the blanket pulled up to her chest, since she didn't have any clothes on. She stared up at him in the dark. "Scott, is that you?"

He reached up and pulled the hood off his face. "God damn fucking right it's me," he spat. "Why couldn't you have just died in the fucking water?"

She shook her head. "It wasn't enough that you pushed me into the water and left us to drown?"

"That storm was a godsend," he said. "Any opportunity to knock you overboard would work for me."

"Why?" she asked. "I didn't do anything to you."

"You broke up with me," he said, "and made me a laughingstock."

"Because I broke off our relationship? Who gave a shit about that?"

He shrugged. "Nobody dumps me," he said. "I'm the one who decides when the relationship is over."

She stared at him in horror. "All of this because I broke up with you, after I found you in bed with another woman, and somehow that's *my* fault, so you're trying to kill me over it?"

Keane could hear the anger rising in her voice. He really loved the spirit in this girl. She'd been through so much and right now was facing a killer head-on instead of backing down and becoming a victim. She was strong and standing firm.

Scott stopped at the end of the bed, but he was still too damn far away, and he was now holding out the handgun. "If you don't shut your fucking mouth," he said, "I'll shoot you right now."

Immediately she closed her mouth and glared at him. She looked around casually. "How did you get in here?"

When her gaze landed on the closet, she caught sight of Keane but drifted past and then came back to look at Scott again. She twisted toward the closet ever-so-slightly, and Scott immediately stepped into her line of vision. Keane realized she'd done that on purpose.

Changing her position caused Scott to move as well, giving Keane a little more opportunity to come out and attack. He really liked that she was staying calm and thinking things through, using her head and trying to help, without giving his position away.

"Nice of your landlord to give me a key," he said, "for the surprise party and all." He cackled at his own joke, sounding deranged.

"Well, I'm leaving this apartment anyway."

"Too bad you didn't leave already," he said.

"Well, if you had your way, I'd already be dead," she snapped. Suddenly she stared at him, slack-jawed. "Jesus. Did you try to kill Brenda too?"

"She saw me push you off the boat," he said.

"Do you know that she saw you, or are you just afraid she might have?"

"I was hoping that I'd have a better position where she wouldn't see me. And I couldn't take a chance, so I figured she had to go anyway."

"Even if she didn't see you push me off? Even if, in the middle of a storm, it was so confusing that nobody knew anything for sure? No matter what, you decided she had to die?"

"Can't have loose ends. They have a habit of coming around and biting you in the ass," he said.

"You realized you failed, right?"

"She's in the hospital," he said. "She's not protected forever. I'll get another chance."

"So this is your second chance to kill me, and you've already tried to kill her once with the hit-and-run. Or did you push her off the damn boat too?"

He just grinned at her.

She stared, stunned. "Seriously?"

"What can I say?" he said. "She was fucking irritating. She was stopping Greg from doing all kinds of shit we used to do together."

"So she didn't fall accidentally?"

"She had a little help," he said. "And you had a little help. That should have been the end of it. Dumped in rough seas in the middle of nowhere with a fucking storm raging. It couldn't have been more perfect."

He shook his head, getting pissed all over again. "But not you. Trust you to end up getting rescued. What are the chances of those smugglers coming along and picking you out of the water and taking you to that island?" He shook his head. "You're always the one who comes up golden."

"Really? Brenda got a bad head injury, Scott. And now I know why. Because you probably hit her over the head when you knocked her over. Didn't you?"

He shrugged.

She took a slow and deep breath. "And, yeah, we got picked up by smugglers, or guys associated with smugglers anyway. We were dropped on a desolate island and locked away in a tiny shelter. Yeah, really lucky. And instead of getting rescued, we ended up in the middle of a drug-smuggling fight with people getting shot all around us. Yeah, so lucky," she murmured.

"Well, that's okay," he said, "because you won't remember any of it by the time I'm done with you."

"And this will be what?" she asked. "Just your average breaking and entering?"

"Why not?" he said. "They happen all the time. I'll make it look like some rapist went crazy, and I'll leave you to die in your little pathetic apartment."

"All because I broke up with you?"

"All because women are bitches," he said, his voice suddenly cheerful. "And because I can."

"So pushing us off the boat gave you a feeling of power. But then fear kicked in, and you realized you hadn't done a good enough job, so now you'll do it all over again. You can feel that power, and you like that feeling, don't you?"

"I sure do," he said. "I'm so damn tired of women taking over the world. Taking my job. Women pretending to be equal to men. Women not doing what they're told." He shook his head. "You should all just fucking die." As he went to lunge at her, Keane jumped from the closet, threw a chokehold around Scott's neck, and, using the same momentum Scott had used to push forward, pushed him to the ground. The gun skidded free and ended up spinning wildly under the bed.

Scott roared, "What the fuck?"

"Yeah, you see your mistake now?" Keane asked. "It was coming here and assuming she was alone."

As soon as he looked up, she had already thrown the nightgown over her head and raced into the kitchen. She came back with zip ties, which they quickly used on Scott's arms and then his legs, while Scott struggled enough that

Keane felt perfectly inclined to give him a couple good hits to the head.

"That's for what you already did," he said, "and this one"—he hit him hard in the ribs—"is for what you were planning on doing. What I *could* do to you for what you've already done would leave you dead, so I'll avoid doing that," he said. "I'm sure jail will take care of you nicely and put you in your place when you become some big man's bitch."

Scott glared at him, and the hate spewing from his mouth had Sandrine racing off again, and she returned with a hand towel and shoved it into his mouth.

"Nobody wants to hear anything you've got to say," she snapped. "I hope they throw you into prison and leave you to rot. Thanks for supplying all the details, by the way." The red Record light on her phone shone brightly.

As she snatched up her phone, Keane looked at her and said, "Grab mine, will you, honey?"

She brought it over to him, and, while he literally sat on Scott's back, Keane dialed Lennox, who answered immediately, having been on alert since Keane's earlier text.

"No need for security at the hospital now," he said. "It was Scott. I've got him tied up here in Sandrine's apartment. And Sandrine got everything recorded. Scott tried to run Brenda down, thinking she had seen him try to kill Sandrine on the sailboat. He's also the one responsible for Brenda going off the boat in the first place. He hit her in the head, knocking her off the boat. That's where her head injury came from."

"What the hell?" Lennox said. "Are you serious?"

"Yeah. Brenda was cramping his style with his buddy Greg apparently."

Keane held the phone by Scott's head and said, "Say something to Lennox, Scott."

All Scott could do was scream his fury through the gag in his mouth.

Lennox laughed. "Okay. I'll be there in a few minutes, and I'll bring the cops with me."

"Yeah, you better. This guy's pissed, and I don't want him to get loose. By the way, he came with a gun too. He was prepared to make it look like a breaking and entering gone bad, a rapist into bondage. He planned to mess her up pretty badly, then walk away in the night. Clearly he hates women, and he's still pissed about that job thing she was telling us about. Remember? When she got the job, and he didn't."

"Wow," Lennox said. "Well, it's pretty easy to know who was the better candidate, right?"

"We sure do," Keane said. After the call, he pocketed his phone and spoke to Sandrine. "You'll probably want to get dressed. Lennox and the cops will be here soon."

She nodded. "It's really over now, isn't it?"

This time her voice was hopeful, but she waited for him to confirm it. He opened his arms, even though he was still sitting on Scott. She shook her head and gestured that he should stand up first. He nodded, and, rising, he walked over and wrapped her in his arms. He whispered, "It's over, and now you get your life back."

She reached up, kissed him and said, "I've got an idea. Since you've already saved my life several times, how about just looking after it from here on out?"

"Instead of me looking after it," he said, "how about we share the responsibility together?"

"That works," she said. "I just want to spend as much time as possible with you."

"Ditto," he said as he leaned over and kissed her once more.

# EPILOGUE

LENNOX CUMMERBUND LANDED just outside of Munich, Germany. He was meeting his sister, Carolina, for a couple days, hoping to get that much time with her before he got called on a mission himself, having finished with Keane's assignment. As Lennox walked out of the airport, his duffel bag over his shoulder, he gazed around, looking to see if she had gotten in before him and was here to pick him up.

A couple days ago they'd made arrangements to fly into the same airport, roughly around the same time. He had her flight number on his phone but hadn't had a confirmation from her that she had managed to catch it. As he walked through one of the lengthy areas of the airport, he saw the computerized flight board above. He quickly checked her flight info. So she should have gotten in about ten minutes before him.

He sent a text her way, saying he would wait outside the front doors near her baggage pickup area. They could grab a cab and head to her apartment that she had here. She was a Red Cross doctor and traveled all over the globe. Breaks off together were hard to come by.

She was his only sibling, and they liked to touch base, if they could, at least once a year. When Lennox received no responding text, he frowned, wondering if Carolina was still stuck on the tarmac, but, even then, they were allowed to turn on their electronics again. He waited inside now, at the luggage pickup. Carousels rolled through for her particular flight. She should arrive here at any time, and, indeed, a crowd had showed up.

He scanned the faces but found no sight of his sister.

His frown deepened, wondering if she couldn't make it. He sent her yet another text; when that didn't work, he dialed her phone number, and his call immediately went to voicemail. Shrugging, he sat at the exit, watching as people came and went. Maybe she got in on an earlier flight, or possibly she was still stuck in whatever godforsaken part of the world she had been in last. He thought it was Somalia.

And given the connecting flights that she probably had to take, she could have been stranded anywhere. Usually she'd send him a message, if that were the case. He checked his email while he was here, but still he had no word from her. Now he was starting to worry.

"Lennox?"

His gaze shot up as he studied the tall dark-haired man in front of him. "Gavin?"

Gavin reached out a hand, and the two shrugged, shook hands, and half hugged in a typical bro manner.

"Damn, it's good to see you," Lennox said. "Odd place, but then, maybe not. I hardly recognized you. You're not in uniform, so you're not here on business?"

"Oh, I'm here on business," Gavin said. The smile fell off his face. "And I'm still in the military, just not the same unit."

"Ah. A lot of that going on. I'm here visiting my sister," Lennox said, holding up his phone. "At least I would be if I could find out what flight she's on or where she got stuck.

Her flight arrived, but she's not on it."

Gavin nodded, his expression turning serious. "That's why I'm here."

Lennox felt something inside him still. "Why?" He straightened his duffel bag at his feet as he glanced around. It seemed everybody suddenly moved slowly, as if only his world had sped up to the point where it all focused entirely on Gavin's face.

"We have reason to believe she's been kidnapped."

This concludes Book 9 of The Mavericks: Keane.
Read about Lennox: The Mavericks, Book 10

# The Mavericks: Lennox (Book #10)

What happens when the very men—trained to make the hard decisions—come up against the rules and regulations that hold them back from doing what needs to be done? They either stay and work within the constraints given to them or they walk away. Only now, for a select few, they have another option:

The Mavericks. A covert black ops team that steps up and break all the rules … but gets the job done.

Welcome to a new military romance series by *USA Today* best-selling author Dale Mayer. A series where you meet new friends and just might get to meet old ones too in this raw and compelling look at the men who keep us safe every day from the darkness where they operate—and live—in the shadows … until someone special helps them step into the light.

**Planning to meet his sister in Germany, but, when she's a no-show, Lennox has his first inkling that trouble has come home in a big way …**

When his sister and her best friend go missing, Lennox is determined to find and to keep his only family member safe … and her best friend. They were both doctors, traveling the globe with the UN. Lennox was proud of his sister's accomplishments. He'd never tried to hide their relationship, thinking no one from Lennox's Navy SEALs past cared—or was still alive. Only now someone has decided to use Lennox's only family as a way to exact revenge.

Helena is caught up in a kidnapping of Lennox's sister, all designed to get back at Lennox—the most infuriating man she's ever met. And one she's cared for since forever. Now to know she was used as a trap to kidnap his sister and to take him out was the worst kind of punishment. But she *knew* this man. Knew him intimately—if only once—but also *knew* he was coming to rescue them, even if it meant losing his own life.

Lennox wasn't letting the only two women in his world be taken out without a fight, … especially one who didn't even know how he felt …

Find book 10 here!
To find out more visit Dale Mayer's website.
https://geni.us/DMLennoxUniversal

# Author's Note

Thank you for reading Keane: The Mavericks, Book 9! If you enjoyed the book, please take a moment and leave a short review.

Dear reader,

I love to hear from readers, and you can contact me at my website: www.dalemayer.com or at my Facebook author page. To be informed of new releases and special offers, sign up for my newsletter or follow me on BookBub. And if you are interested in joining Dale Mayer's Reader Group, here is the Facebook sign up page.
http://geni.us/DaleMayerFBGroup

Cheers,
Dale Mayer

# About the Author

Dale Mayer is a *USA Today* best-selling author, best known for her SEALs military romances, her Psychic Visions series, and her Lovely Lethal Garden cozy series. Her contemporary romances are raw and full of passion and emotion (Broken But … Mending, Hathaway House series). Her thrillers will keep you guessing (Kate Morgan, By Death series), and her romantic comedies will keep you giggling (*It's a Dog's Life*, a stand-alone novella; and the Broken Protocols series, starring Charming Marvin, the cat).

Dale honors the stories that come to her—and some of them are crazy, break all the rules and cross multiple genres!

To go with her fiction, she also writes nonfiction in many different fields, with books available on résumé writing, companion gardening, and the US mortgage system. All her books are available in print and ebook format.

## Connect with Dale Mayer Online

*Dale's Website – www.dalemayer.com*

*Twitter – @DaleMayer*

*Facebook Page – geni.us/DaleMayerFBFanPage*

*Facebook Group – geni.us/DaleMayerFBGroup*

*BookBub – geni.us/DaleMayerBookbub*

*Instagram – geni.us/DaleMayerInstagram*

*Goodreads – geni.us/DaleMayerGoodreads*

*Newsletter – geni.us/DaleNews*

# Also by Dale Mayer

## Published Adult Books:

**Hathaway House**
Aaron, Book 1
Brock, Book 2
Cole, Book 3
Denton, Book 4
Elliot, Book 5
Finn, Book 6
Gregory, Book 7
Heath, Book 8
Iain, Book 9

**The K9 Files**
Ethan, Book 1
Pierce, Book 2
Zane, Book 3
Blaze, Book 4
Lucas, Book 5
Parker, Book 6
Carter, Book 7

**Lovely Lethal Gardens**
Arsenic in the Azaleas, Book 1
Bones in the Begonias, Book 2
Corpse in the Carnations, Book 3
Daggers in the Dahlias, Book 4

Evidence in the Echinacea, Book 5
Footprints in the Ferns, Book 6
Gun in the Gardenias, Book 7
Handcuffs in the Heather, Book 8
Ice Pick in the Ivy, Book 9

## Psychic Vision Series

Tuesday's Child
Hide 'n Go Seek
Maddy's Floor
Garden of Sorrow
Knock Knock…
Rare Find
Eyes to the Soul
Now You See Her
Shattered
Into the Abyss
Seeds of Malice
Eye of the Falcon
Itsy-Bitsy Spider
Unmasked
Deep Beneath
From the Ashes
Stroke of Death
Psychic Visions Books 1–3
Psychic Visions Books 4–6
Psychic Visions Books 7–9

## By Death Series

Touched by Death
Haunted by Death
Chilled by Death
By Death Books 1–3

## Broken Protocols – Romantic Comedy Series

Cat's Meow
Cat's Pajamas
Cat's Cradle
Cat's Claus
Broken Protocols 1-4

## Broken and… Mending

Skin
Scars
Scales (of Justice)
Broken but… Mending 1-3

## Glory

Genesis
Tori
Celeste
Glory Trilogy

## Biker Blues

Morgan: Biker Blues, Volume 1
Cash: Biker Blues, Volume 2

## SEALs of Honor

Mason: SEALs of Honor, Book 1
Hawk: SEALs of Honor, Book 2
Dane: SEALs of Honor, Book 3
Swede: SEALs of Honor, Book 4
Shadow: SEALs of Honor, Book 5
Cooper: SEALs of Honor, Book 6
Markus: SEALs of Honor, Book 7
Evan: SEALs of Honor, Book 8
Mason's Wish: SEALs of Honor, Book 9

Chase: SEALs of Honor, Book 10
Brett: SEALs of Honor, Book 11
Devlin: SEALs of Honor, Book 12
Easton: SEALs of Honor, Book 13
Ryder: SEALs of Honor, Book 14
Macklin: SEALs of Honor, Book 15
Corey: SEALs of Honor, Book 16
Warrick: SEALs of Honor, Book 17
Tanner: SEALs of Honor, Book 18
Jackson: SEALs of Honor, Book 19
Kanen: SEALs of Honor, Book 20
Nelson: SEALs of Honor, Book 21
Taylor: SEALs of Honor, Book 22
Colton: SEALs of Honor, Book 23
Troy: SEALs of Honor, Book 24
SEALs of Honor, Books 1–3
SEALs of Honor, Books 4–6
SEALs of Honor, Books 7–10
SEALs of Honor, Books 11–13
SEALs of Honor, Books 14–16
SEALs of Honor, Books 17–19

**Heroes for Hire**
Levi's Legend: Heroes for Hire, Book 1
Stone's Surrender: Heroes for Hire, Book 2
Merk's Mistake: Heroes for Hire, Book 3
Rhodes's Reward: Heroes for Hire, Book 4
Flynn's Firecracker: Heroes for Hire, Book 5
Logan's Light: Heroes for Hire, Book 6
Harrison's Heart: Heroes for Hire, Book 7
Saul's Sweetheart: Heroes for Hire, Book 8
Dakota's Delight: Heroes for Hire, Book 9

Michael's Mercy (Part of Sleeper SEAL Series)
Tyson's Treasure: Heroes for Hire, Book 10
Jace's Jewel: Heroes for Hire, Book 11
Rory's Rose: Heroes for Hire, Book 12
Brandon's Bliss: Heroes for Hire, Book 13
Liam's Lily: Heroes for Hire, Book 14
North's Nikki: Heroes for Hire, Book 15
Anders's Angel: Heroes for Hire, Book 16
Reyes's Raina: Heroes for Hire, Book 17
Dezi's Diamond: Heroes for Hire, Book 18
Vince's Vixen: Heroes for Hire, Book 19
Ice's Icing: Heroes for Hire, Book 20
Johan's Joy: Heroes for Hire, Book 21
Heroes for Hire, Books 1–3
Heroes for Hire, Books 4–6
Heroes for Hire, Books 7–9
Heroes for Hire, Books 10–12
Heroes for Hire, Books 13–15

## SEALs of Steel

Badger: SEALs of Steel, Book 1
Erick: SEALs of Steel, Book 2
Cade: SEALs of Steel, Book 3
Talon: SEALs of Steel, Book 4
Laszlo: SEALs of Steel, Book 5
Geir: SEALs of Steel, Book 6
Jager: SEALs of Steel, Book 7
The Final Reveal: SEALs of Steel, Book 8
SEALs of Steel, Books 1–4
SEALs of Steel, Books 5–8
SEALs of Steel, Books 1–8

## The Mavericks

Kerrick, Book 1

Griffin, Book 2

Jax, Book 3

Beau, Book 4

Asher, Book 5

Ryker, Book 6

Miles, Book 7

Nico, Book 8

Keane, Book 9

Lennox, Book 10

Gavin, Book 11

Shane, Book 12

## Bullard's Battle Series

Ryland's Reach, Book 1

Cain's Cross, Book 2

Eton's Escape, Book 3

Garret's Gambit, Book 4

Kano's Keep, Book 5

Fallon's Flaw, Book 6

Quinn's Quest, Book 7

Bullard's Beauty, Book 8

## Collections

Dare to Be You…

Dare to Love…

Dare to be Strong…

RomanceX3

## Standalone Novellas

It's a Dog's Life

Riana's Revenge

Second Chances

# Published Young Adult Books:

## Family Blood Ties Series

Vampire in Denial

Vampire in Distress

Vampire in Design

Vampire in Deceit

Vampire in Defiance

Vampire in Conflict

Vampire in Chaos

Vampire in Crisis

Vampire in Control

Vampire in Charge

Family Blood Ties Set 1–3

Family Blood Ties Set 1–5

Family Blood Ties Set 4–6

Family Blood Ties Set 7–9

Sian's Solution, A Family Blood Ties Series Prequel
Novelette

## Design series

Dangerous Designs

Deadly Designs

Darkest Designs

Design Series Trilogy

## Standalone

In Cassie's Corner

Gem Stone (a Gemma Stone Mystery)

Time Thieves

# Published Non-Fiction Books:

**Career Essentials**

Career Essentials: The Résumé

Career Essentials: The Cover Letter

Career Essentials: The Interview

Career Essentials: 3 in 1

www.ingramcontent.com/pod-product-compliance
Lightning Source LLC
Chambersburg PA
CBHW071358100726
47908CB00004B/1036